Haunts and Howls Collections

Haunts and Howls and Guardian Spells
Haunts and Howls Where Demons Dwell
Haunts and Howls and Jesters Bells
Haunts and Howls and Fairy Dales

HAUNTS AND HOWLS AND FAIRY DALES

A CONTEMPORARY FANTASY COLLECTION

KAT SIMONS

HAUNTS AND HOWLS AND FAIRY DALES

CONTENTS

For my mom and dad
Who introduced me to fairytales and Irish legends.

For my husband
Who keeps me grounded.

And for my boys
Who keep me entertained.

INTRODUCTION

Fairytales have been a part of my life since I was a child and they have had a profound impact on my love of fantasy fiction. The older I got, the more I enjoyed the scarier versions of those fairytales, too. Fairies in general are hard to resist, mythical beings that can take many forms, inspire love and fear in equal measure, be the epitome of evil or goodness, and can mean a lot of different things to the people who tell stories about them.

The tales I read as a kid were mostly informed by European fairies (I'm looking at you Grimm Brothers), so those are the ones I'm most familiar with. I love *all* fairies and fairy stories, but I've had the most exposure to the European Fae. And in particular, I've always had a soft spot for Irish myths and legends, especially around the Fae.

Which is going to be very obvious in this collection because most of the stories touch on or reference Irish Fae—I only realized how often I "go to" Ireland to tell a fairy story after I started putting the collection together and all but two of the stories had something to do with Ireland. Out of the seven included here, three take place in Ireland and two reference Irish mythology.

Obviously, my subconscious loves Irish fairytales.

Two of the stories here are also older, written years ago. One, a short piece that's almost a prose poem, I wrote while I was living in Germany for a year, where I was soaking up a lot of Black Forest mythology. The other, I wrote while living in Ireland, when I was steeped in Irish legends and reading a lot of books—both fiction and non-fiction—about all things Irish. That wasn't why I was in Ireland. I was there to get my Ph.D. in animal behavior. But I still spent a lot of time soaking up all the cultural legends I could.

The two stories I wrote all those years ago aren't things I would probably write now, at least not in the way they're written. I'm not so immersed in the lyrical world of myths and local legends anymore, and the distance means the stories come out differently now. But the ones I wrote during that period of time still hold up, and they are a perfect fit to this collection.

The poem that follows this introduction is also one of the very few poems I've ever written—well, outside of that period in my teenage years when all the angst resulted in some truly horrific poetry. I didn't keep those, though. This poem I kept. For most of my writing life, I've been primarily a prose person. But this particular poem came out of me during this Irish fairytale immersion period, and it fits this collection so perfectly, I couldn't leave it out. Plus, I really love it. I might not write poetry often (as a much less angsty adult), but the few that tumble out of my fingers tend to really stick with me.

There are also some old friends in these pages. In fact, the very first story in the collection, *The Red Fear Pipes*, takes us back to Friday's Curious Shop. This one is both a bit creepy and also very indicative of the chaos fairies are wont to cause. Because of course the mischievous and chaotic fairies find their way to Friday's.

The next story is one of those older stories, the prose poem. *Sings the Forest* is short, more like a flash fiction piece, but it packs an emotional punch.

Following that, I have three stories in a row that are set in Ireland. The first, *Black Water Hawthorns*, is set on a fictionalized version of my old college campus in Dublin. The campus has changed a lot since my years there, so this is almost historical because it's the campus as I remember it, and takes place in that time period. I can't say more about it, though, without giving something away. But just be reassured, this did not happen to me while I was there. I promise I'm making it up. Really. Promise.

After that, another of the older stories. This one told from a "storyteller's" point of view and very much in the voice of Ireland of old. *The Fairies and the Brier* had a lot of heavy influence from all the myths I was reading back in the day, and, to me anyway, feels like something that could have shown up in a "Book of Irish Myths" collections. I made this one up, of course, but I wanted it to feel like that. Hopefully, I succeeded.

The third of this Ireland set trilogy, and fifth story in the collection, *To Dance in Fallow Fields at Midnight*, takes a character I can very much relate to, a writer, and gives her all those "quaint Ireland" ideas that a lot of Americans have about the country. The romanticized version of a place and actually living in a place are two very different things, and as someone who's lived in some interesting places, I knew this going in when I moved to Ireland. But I still met a lot of Americans who had very romantic ideas of the country. Taking those starry-eyed dreams and combining them with some spooky fairy stuff was a lot of fun. Spooky is, after all, the name of the game with a Haunts and Howls collection.

Next up is something completely different because of course I have to have something completely different in a Haunts and Howls collection, too. *The Troll and the Dressmaker* sees readers into a fairytale world where the secondary characters, those ordinary people living in villages, get a story. A story that introduces a familiar "monster" and a unique one as well.

And finally, we meet another old friend in the final novella of the collection. *Cary at the Crossroads* sees magical Protector Cary Redmond and her faery mentor Jaxer facing off against some pretty spooky Fae, with a twist on the tale of the beings you might meet at midnight at a crossroads. I couldn't resist writing a story with Cary for this collection because so much of her life is influenced by the Fae, even if she sometimes forgets that part. For anyone reading the Cary Redmond urban fantasy series, this story takes place about two or three weeks before the start of The Trouble with Black Cats and Demons, the very first novel in the series, so there are a few easter eggs dropped at the very end. Bwah ha ha.

Scary, spooky, chaotic, mischievous, fun, and lyrical, fairies provided so many opportunities for me as a storyteller. This collection definitely reveals my Irish leanings, and was a seriously fun collection to write and put together. I hope readers will enjoy these trips into the dales where fairy's dance, and strange things slip through that thin veil between our reality and the world of the Fae.

Thanks for reading.

Kat Simons
October 2024

Have you seen the fairies' flight
about the fires late at night?
They dance and sing the evenings through,
Then on they race till the moon be blue;
And on that bright and fiery eve,
Their wings alight with rainbow hues,
The fairy dance at last will stop
For a heartbeat's length,
and then they're off.

THE RED FEAR PIPES

A FRIDAY'S CURIOUS SHOP STORY

*R*iley stared at her boss, Doreen Sinclair, for a long moment, wondering why the simple request to go dust the children's toy section of the secondhand store filled her with such dread. She always dusted every part of the store. That was part of her job at Friday's Curious Shop. Deal with customers. Help Doreen and Ian—the brother and sister who owned the store—when they needed it. Dust things.

The dusting never seemed to take for very long, so there was always plenty of it to do.

Something about all the clutter and chaos of tables and shelves and cases stacked tightly together and filled with everything from used tools to elegant scarves. The Queens store, with only a vague sort of organization to all that stuff, seemed to attract dust. Could be the elevated subway that ran past a few blocks away. Or the location, which was on a strange, off-the-beaten-path block not far from a bunch of storage unit businesses—not a place one would normally think a retail story, even a secondhand retail store, would choose. Somehow, they still got enough walk-ins and regular customers to stay in business.

Riley wasn't sure how that all worked, honestly. She helped customers from time-to-time, but a lot of her days seemed to be dusting and rearranging and eating the sandwiches Ian Sinclair often treated them all to for lunch.

But her pay always turned up in her bank account on time every two weeks, no matter how much business the shop seemed to get. That, all on its own, had made taking this job worthwhile. She'd been just about homeless when she'd applied for the sales clerk position here, and since starting, she'd been able to not only afford to keep a roof over her head and pay her part of the rent, she now had health insurance and had been able to get a new contact lens prescription for the first time in two years.

Friday's Curious Shop might be a little strange, but this place had saved her from living on the streets. Probably saved her life. This job was worth everything to her. Even if a lot of her time was spent rearranging displays, folding shirts, straightening magazines, attempting to stack mismatched kitchen wares, or moving and removing stacks of maybe-valuable paintings. And dusting. Lots of dusting. Which, every so often, meant dusting the toy section.

But today, for reasons she couldn't entirely place, dusting the toy section filled her with near panic. She *did not* want to go into that part of the story.

So weird.

"You okay?" Doreen asked, looking up from the catalogue she was reviewing, pushing her large, electric blue-framed glasses up her nose.

Doreen had a great collection of glasses and seemed to be wearing a new pair every few weeks. She was perched behind the raised wooden register counter, a common place for her to spend quiet moments, going through a catalogue of collectible glassware. Her curly red hair was pulled back today in a low ponytail, and she wore a deep purple sweater over black trousers. Unlike her brother's more flamboyant dress sense, Doreen leaned toward more conservative looks, but usually with one interesting pattern or one element of softness in her clothing. Today, that was the cashmere sweater that looked fuzzy and cozy.

"Fine," Riley said, trying to force a smile. "My allergies are acting up today. Dusting sounds painful."

Doreen nodded and sighed. "I understand. I keep hoping Ian will invent something that keeps this place permanently dusted." She gave Riley a considering look, her brown eyes huge behind her thick lenses, her light makeup accenting her freckles rather than hiding them. "You want to give dusting a miss today? Not like the dust won't be there tomorrow."

"No, it's fine. I'll take care of it." The Sinclairs were so good to her, Riley hated not doing anything they asked her to do around the shop. It felt disloyal. "I'll just hold my breath," she joked.

"Don't do that. If you pass out, it might take us a week to find you!" Doreen smiled as she joked, but there was an edge of concern under the joke that surprised Riley.

"Okay," she said. "No breath-holding. Just an extra allergy pill at lunch." She grabbed the duster handle from behind the counter and slid on a fresh puff that would hopefully catch more of the dust and dirt than it sent scattering. Then headed into the toy section, steeling her spine. She'd dusted there before. There was no reason to feel nervous.

Still, as she neared the case of musical jewelry boxes, the top one opened to reveal a ballerina, frozen en pointe, Riley paused, her pulse racing. She pressed a hand to her chest to try and convince her heartbeat there was no reason to be so nervous.

She stared at the glass case, at the music boxes.

Some were old and looked pretty beat up. She wasn't even sure why they were kept in a case. Chipped paint, worn wood, the musical element missing or broken. But some of them were really beautiful.

There was one with a green pearlescent inlay, with swirls of gold inside the green giving the box a shimmer. And the blue painted wooden box that looked like a miniature wardrobe from Versailles, complete with gold leaf details. There was the dark blue Wedgewood box that Riley was certain was worth a small fortune, though the price tag said fifty bucks. And the cut crystal box with the musical element visible through the rainbow prism of light that reflected on all the decorative angles.

The sheer hodge podge of boxes was astounding. And there was no rhyme or reason to their organization in the case. The beautiful ones were shelved next to the worn ones, the antique next to the modern mass-produced.

Her favorite box in the case was probably the simple dark wood box with an inlaid cut of lighter wood formed into a tree on the lid. There were lines of green running through the wood that looked a little like gemstones. And when the box caught the light just right, it almost looked like it was glowing.

She'd never seen the inside of the box. It had always remained inside the case and no one had asked to see it. She couldn't even remember when the Sinclairs had added it to the collection. It hadn't been there in her first few weeks at Friday's. But she'd admired it after it had appeared.

How long had it been there now? She couldn't remember. There was always so much that came in and went out of the store. Given how few customers came in, she was always surprised by the regular changes in stock. She suspected Ian and Doreen moved items from the back out front and from the front to the back regularly, to make it look like things were changing more than they actually were.

She took her duster to the glass on the music box case, hesitant to move deeper into the toy section. Most of the toys were just used, modern things with missing pieces and well-worn edges. The sort of things you'd find at a charity shop. Sometimes there was a valuable piece, an original China doll, a board game that was out of print, a collection of marbles with actual valuable marbles inside. But mostly, it was just junk as far as Riley could tell.

The doll collection had always made her nervous. All those eyes watching her as she dusted.

But she'd never had this visceral a need to remain outside that part of the store. It wasn't just her allergies. Something in the shadows was giving her the creeps. Something that wasn't the dolls was…

Watching her.

The sense of being watched made her shiver.

She focused on the music boxes, on her favorite box, and tried not to notice the crawl of dread along her spine, the shiver of fear over her shoulders, the way the hair on the back of her neck prickled and raised.

No. Everything was fine. Just the usual low-level weirdness of dead dolls' eyes staring at her. Everyone thought that was freaky. Honestly, she didn't know what little kids saw in dolls. There wasn't one she'd ever seen that didn't feel mildly sinister.

But the sense of dread and fear wasn't coming from the pile of dolls. It was coming from darker shadows near a collection of toy instruments.

She'd never been bothered by the toy instruments before. The battery-operated, blue plastic microphone didn't really work anymore but it was cute. The plastic drum set would be some poor parent's bane one day. The little triangles, the wooden recorders her grandmother had claimed were a rite of passage at school in her day, the ukulele that looked more authentic than some of the other things.

She remained by the music box case, but frowned as she realized there was a new instrument among the other toys. A little multi-piped flute thing. She wasn't sure what they were called, but they reminded her of the instrument Pan was shown playing in old paintings. Like an old-fashioned harmonica or something.

Riley edged closer. That flute thing hadn't been there a few days ago, had it? If she'd seen it before, she'd have taken the time to learn what it was called, or asked Doreen or Ian about it. Probably just called pipes, she thought with an inward groan.

It actually looked well-made and authentic. Not a worn plastic toy. It was made of small, hollow wooden cylinders held together by a strip of metal that had an elegant design of Celtic knots and swirls. In the middle of the design work, she swore she saw small creatures, though she was too far away to see what kind of animal those smaller images might be. And if she turned her head just right, the metal band around the pipes seemed to shimmer with a sort of purplish-blue light. Really more purple than blue.

Very pretty actually.

She absently brushed her duster over the glass case, but turned her full attention to the pipes.

She could almost hear music.

CHAPTER 2

Riley listened to the noise coming from the pipes curiously. It really did sound like music. Likely it was just the air moving through the store blowing through the pipes, creating sound. But the sound was surprisingly melodious given it had to be a fluke of random air currents.

She edged closer to the pipes as she dusted a pile of board games stacked on a table near the music box display case. The pipes' music seemed even more like music now, but a discordant music. Something just a little off about it, yet it was a definite tune.

So strange.

The sound grated against her ears, though. Made her edgy and irritated. Like someone was poking her in the ears with tiny fire sticks. She wasn't going to be able to stay in the area dusting with that noise.

She reached for the flute thing to move it somewhere the air currents wouldn't get to it, or maybe tuck it under a pile of stuffed animals or something, but she hesitated with her hand in the air, just above it. And shivered.

The feeling reminded her of when she had to lift a

garbage lid in her building's basement to throw stuff away and she just *knew* on an instinctive level that there would be a cockroach somewhere on that lid, and the fucker would jump out and run right past her hand the minute she touched the lid. This moment felt like that. Like the moment she touched the pipes, something would skitter across her hand like a cockroach.

Fisting her hand in the air once, she released her hesitance with an irritated snort. She had never once seen a cockroach in this store—which was a little surprising now that she thought about it—or a mouse for that matter. And it was just a child's toy. It wasn't going to jump up and bite her.

She snatched at the pipes.

And to her utter astonishment, the pipes leapt away.

Riley stared wide-eyed at the wooden instrument laying a few feet from where it had previously been, still issuing that irritating music, that discordant sound of air through the little round wooden tubes. The decorative metal strap that lashed the cylinders together flared with that strange purple color. Or so Riley thought as she stared. But that could have just been a trick of the light.

The fact that the pipes had *moved* on its own was not a trick of the light.

It had to be a trick, though, right? Maybe a jumping cockroach? The water bugs could be huge. Maybe big enough to carry a wooden set of pipes on their back and move it on accident?

Or maybe it was something larger, like a mouse, and it had somehow gotten the pipes attached to its back?

She shivered. She wasn't mad about mice. And she loathed cockroaches.

But they were the only logical explanation, so it had to be

one of them. Did she try to pick up the pipes again or did she go get Ian like a proper wuss?

She was leaning toward Ian. In fact, an instinct was pushing her to go get one of the siblings. To not do this on her own. But do *what* exactly? She wasn't sure. Picking up a set of flying pipes shouldn't feel this complicated. But also, pipes shouldn't fly. So she felt justified in her low level terror.

She knew coming to this area to dust today was a mistake. *Knew it.*

Though, honestly, she still wasn't sure why it was a mistake.

The pipes' discordant music hit her nerves again, like tiny spikes, and she came close to holding her hands over her ears to block the sound. That felt childish but also she was in the toy section so also appropriate.

The pipes moved again and Riley jumped, dropping the nearly forgotten duster in her hand.

That wasn't an air current. There were no air currents in this place that would move something as substantial as the pipes like that.

Riley's mind skittered up to a vague memory of the storage room behind the store, a space that always seemed so much bigger than it could possibly be. She didn't go back there alone. In fact, she rarely went back there ever. Maybe… two or three times in all the months she'd worked at Friday's. She thought anyway. She only had a sort of vague image of the back room that she could pull from her memory. So obviously, she hadn't been back there very much if she could barely remember what it looked like.

None of which had anything to do with the jumping pipes, except for maybe the fact that she thought Ian might be in the storage room. He hadn't gone out for lunch yet. He wasn't at the desk with Doreen, and he rarely—almost never

—went into the office to one side of the register desk. That was Doreen's domain.

Riley was pretty sure she'd seen Ian that morning when she came in to work. She didn't think he was off on one of his trips to get more stuff for the store. She felt like she'd remember that. But if he wasn't poking around the main floor with one of his drones, or at the back desk or office, there was nowhere else for him to be but the storage room behind the registration desk.

Where she wasn't going to go without Doreen. So getting Doreen would be best.

She didn't want to look away from the pipes, though, so she backed away, moving slowly so she didn't upend a table or display case and accidently startled whatever was under those pipes into moving. She was certain if the pipes jumped again, she'd scream. And if it was just a cockroach or mouse, or—worse!—a rat, she'd be a little embarrassed that she'd screamed. Not enough to stand her ground against a New York rat. She'd be standing on the register counter so fast, Doreen would think she materialized there.

She had reached the glass case with the music boxes when a whispered sound stopped her retreat.

"Riley…"

So quietly, she could barely hear it. So quiet, she was sure she was hearing it wrong. The noise seemed to be coming from the pipes, and so it had to be a trick of the air moving through the musical instrument.

Another whispered, "Riley…"

Yeah, no, she was getting Ian. Now. She had no idea what was happening with those pipes, but the fact that they were now making a noise that sounded like her name was a last straw.

She turned to run to the rear of the store.
And ran smack into a solid wall of muscle.

CHAPTER 3

$\mathcal{R}$iley sputtered and jumped back, thinking she'd run into her bear of a boss. Apologies sprang to her lips and heat crawled up her neck. Ian was a big man who moved entirely too quietly through the store. Where Riley had to worry about bumping into things, Ian somehow managed to navigate this place like he *wasn't* a bull in a China shop.

But when she looked up, she realized she wasn't looking at Ian. That the wall of muscle belonged to a stranger. A man who was roughly the size of Ian in width but wasn't actually quite as tall. He was extremely handsome, though. That sort of unreal, soap opera star handsome that wasn't supposed to exist in real life. Dark hair, green eyes, chiseled jaw. All the symmetry in face and body.

Riley suppressed a shiver. Not a happy sexy shiver, though. The man instantly set her on edge and made her nervous.

This was not the first time she'd encountered a customer who made her nervous, but this was probably the first time a male model had walked into Friday's and set Riley's teeth on edge.

To be fair, a male model had never walked into Friday's since she'd been working there. But still.

She forced a smile, which the man returned politely, but with some restraint. "Sorry about that," she said. "May I help you with something?"

The man's gaze jumped between her and the pipes, then back to her. "Just looking around. Thanks."

She nodded, still so embarrassed about bumping into him that it took her another beat to remember she hadn't heard the bell over the door that announced when a customer entered the shop. Probably just missed the sound over the weird music coming from the pipes. Which…

Were silent now.

She glanced back at instrument. It was still where it had last leapt, nestled in a pile of stuffed animals. But whatever air current had started it making noise had shifted because the pipes were now silent. She wasn't hearing that eerie sound like someone saying her name anymore either.

Maybe all that had just been her imagination.

Though, the pipes had definitely moved. A couple of times. There had to be some sort of vermin around here that had made it move. Which meant she'd better go warn Doreen and Ian.

To the customer, she said, "If you need any help, just let us know."

"Us?"

"My bosses are around here somewhere," she said, forcing a smile she hoped came off professionally. Hard to say for sure. Her face felt stiff and her skin hot and itchy. She was sure that was just the embarrassment.

"Thank you," the man said, his gaze moving back to the pipes. Dismissing her.

She took the excuse, and the dismissal, to hurry away. Happy to put some distance between herself and the pipes anyway. She picked up her dropped duster, gave the glass case with the music boxes a final dust for show, and headed toward the register desk.

Behind her, she swore she heard giggling. A high-pitched giggle. Not the sort of sound she'd have expected from the man, but you never knew.

When she reached the back of the store, Ian was standing next to the counter, messing with the remote control to one of his small drones. He was always tinkering with the mini-kamikaze machines, but the machines were determined to throw themselves into the nearest pile of breakables every time he turned them on.

Ian was the more flamboyant dresser of the siblings. Well, not so much flamboyant as very specific in his style. And that style involved pants that had patterns on them, a button-down dress shirt, and a vest over the shirt. Usually with a tartan pattern but occasionally the vest was dotted with little fleur-de-lis or paisley patterns.

Today, he was almost somber in dark slacks with a pinstripe and a green tartan vest. His shirt was a little rumpled and his sleeves were rolled up. His red beard was neatly trimmed and he'd recently gotten a haircut to tame his wild red hair.

Riley hurried up to the siblings and lowered her voice, even though the customer was far enough away he wasn't likely to hear her. "We have a customer. And we might have a mouse or cockroach or something."

Doreen scowled, an expression that pushed her glasses down her nose. "Did you see one?"

"No. But a set of…I can't remember what they're called. That musical instrument that Pan runs around with. The series of wooden cylinders banded together with a metal strap?"

"Reed pipes," Doreen said.

"Oh. Huh. I've been calling them pipes, but I thought I was wrong."

"What did the pipes look like?" Ian asked.

Riley shrugged. "Little wooden tubes with a single metal band around them. The band was pretty, decorated in Celtic knots. It caught the light funny and looked like it was glowing purple."

Ian and Doreen exchanged a look. "The pipes moved?"

Riley nodded and shivered. "Sorry. I just don't like mice. Or cockroaches."

"Fair enough," Ian said, still holding Doreen's gaze.

"Was the customer inordinately beautiful?" Doreen asked without looking away from Ian. "Like, the kind of beauty you don't normally encounter in real life?"

"Yes!" Riley leaned in and lowered her voice further. "I was thinking he might be one of the soap stars or something. Too handsome to be real."

"Showed interest in the pipes, did he?" Ian said.

Riley nodded. "What's going on?"

Doreen let out a breath, her brows creased, her mouth tense. Ian glanced toward the side of the shop where Riley had left the customer. They both looked grim.

"Think we've got an infestation," Ian said finally.

"Mice? Roaches?" Riley swallowed hard. "Rats?"

"Worse," Ian said.

He and Doreen exchanged another look. Then they both headed toward the toy section of the shop.

Riley looked between them and the relative safety of the register counter. She could stay here, mind the register until

Doreen got back. That made sense. And would put her half the store away from any mice.

But Ian had said it was worse than mice. Or even rats. What the hell kind of infestation were they talking about?

She looked between the retreating backs of her bosses and the desk, then back to the spot where her bosses had disappeared into the stacks of stuff.

A shiver crawled along her spine. And she'd swear she heard that eerie pipe sound, all the way back here. "Riley…"

Imagination. She was sure of it.

But did she really want to be alone with her imagination right then?

Her brain said get behind the counter and mind the cash register.

Her body took her back into the store, following Ian and Doreen to the toy section. And whatever might be an infestation worse than rats.

CHAPTER 4

By the time Riley reached the others, Doreen, Ian, and the too-handsome-to-be-real man were all standing side by side, looking at the pipes. It was no longer sitting on top of a pile of stuffed animals, but had somehow migrated to a stack of tin boxes. Which made the sound coming from the pipes echo and made the discordant noise even eerier.

Riley stopped beside Doreen and whispered, "What's happening?" She had no idea why she was whispering outside of the fact that no one else was speaking. Except the pipes. The pipes were "speaking." But that didn't really count since it wasn't telling them much.

"Infestation," Doreen said with a sigh. "They never come in here. Why now?"

"I've been tracking these for a few days," the too-handsome man said. "Maybe they thought your store would be safe?"

"Or you wouldn't come in to get them out," Ian said, his voice a deep rumble. And the Scottish accent that rarely surfaced sounded stronger.

Riley had heard Ian's faint Scottish burr maybe twice before. Mostly, he just sounded like an American. It was interesting to hear the accent now, and she wondered at it.

"I haven't been barred," the man said. "From this store anyway. Your cousin's store…" The man gave a little shrug.

Riley blinked at the man. Cousin? This was the first she'd heard of the Sinclairs having a cousin with a store like Friday's. Or maybe the cousin's store was something different.

"He'd welcome the bloody fear dearg," Doreen said with a snarl.

"Far darg?" Riley asked, trying to wrap her tongue around the way Doreen had pronounced the two words. She was still trying to catch up after learning her bosses had a cousin with a similar shop that they'd never mentioned before. But this stranger who looked like he belonged on a movie screen knew about the cousin and their store.

Doreen gestured at the humming pipes. "Little feckers are a pain in the ass if they get in. Worse than imps."

"Imps?"

"Could be worse," the man said. "Could be one of the goblins."

Doreen snort-laughed. "I'd take a goblin any day over the fear dearg. Fear dearg bite."

"Wait, something bites?" Riley moved a little behind Doreen. "Is far…fear dearg, like, the species name of a rat or something?" Rats carried rabies, too, didn't they? Or was she misremembering that.

The pipes' weird music got louder, and what sounded like laughter ran around the store, in a rapid echo that reminded Riley of an IMAX theater.

She spun to follow the sound. The others readjusted their positions. And somehow, they all ended up standing back-to-back in a small circle, everyone facing a different part of the shop. Like they were facing something very dangerous and guarding each other's backs.

The instinctiveness of it all felt very ominous to Riley.

The laughter raced around them again. Grating and sharp. Then a hissing sound. Then the pipes again. This time louder and even more tuneless than before.

"What's happening?" Riley whispered, her gaze jumping around the store, following the laughter and pipe music. The pipe itself wasn't moving around. But the sound of the music was now. And the laughter flitted around them chaotically, never coming from the same spot.

"The red men," Doreen said with a sigh. "Like I said. An infestation."

"Did they bring the pipe in? I hadn't seen it before." Not that that was unusual in Friday's. Things seemed to appear out of nowhere all the time. There was so much stuff, moving one thing could often reveal something that had been hidden.

Or at least, that's what she told herself to explain the sudden appearance of new items.

Ian sighed loudly. "The flute's what let them in." He mumbled something Riley couldn't hear.

She wanted to ask more questions, but suddenly the laugher was closer, more insistent, almost…angry?

How could laughter be angry?

If it was possible, this was the laughter that could do it. Definitely didn't sound like happy laughter at any rate.

The sound of glass breaking made Ian curse. The too-handsome man let out a long sigh. Doreen grunted something about insurance.

The part of Riley's brain that wasn't terrified was irritated that she'd have to clean up whatever mess was being made.

But honestly, most of her brain was just terrified.

Another crash. This time toppling the pile of dolls so close to Riley she jumped backward and nearly knocked over Ian, who turned enough to catch her. Once she had her balance, Ian faced outward again.

One of the dolls rolled close to Riley, looking up at her with its dead doll eyes. That did not help her nerves.

From the music box case to her left, one of the boxes started to play, the ballerina inside spinning in a strange sort of disjointed turn, like there was something wrong with the mechanism.

Then another box started to play. The two different songs didn't blend even a little bit. Adding new levels of discordant noise to the sound of pipes whirling around them.

A third box started to play. And then a fourth.

"Now what?" Doreen snapped over the mayhem. "We don't have the cualthan here to clear them out."

"I've got one," the too-handsome man said. "But we have to corner them. Round them up into one place. If even one gets away, the cualthan won't work."

"Of course not," Doreen said.

She sounded so disgusted and irritated, Riley could almost believe this was more like a mice infestation than something so terrifyingly freaky it was making Riley's heart hammer through her chest.

If Doreen wasn't freaking out, though, then it couldn't be that bad, right?

Another music box joined the cacophony. The sounds so disjointed now, it wasn't even pretending to be music anymore. Not even close. Just screeching and screaming and moaning. Like the sounds of a car wreck.

"How do we corner them?" Ian asked the man.

"You wouldn't happen to have a Antashi box?"

"A what?" Riley asked. She wasn't sure she'd heard him right over all the noise.

"Antashi box. Made from the Tree of Life," the man answered off-handedly.

Riley assumed "made from the tree of life" was either a euphemism or a reference to the manufacturer's brand.

"You just need a box?" she asked. "We have lots of those."

"Needs to be a special kind. The wood will look like its glowing. There will be green lines running through it that almost look like jewels. And somewhere on it, there will be a Tree of Life design."

"Like the box in the case?" She gestured toward the glass display case where a great deal of the noise was coming from.

Ian spun around. "There's an Antashi case in there?"

"When did you first see it?" Doreen asked, sounding urgent. "When did it arrive?"

She talked about it "arriving" as if it had just walked in.

"I…can't remember. I remember looking at it today when I was dusting. I like it. It's one of the nicer music boxes we have. I was thinking today that it was my favorite in the case, so I must have seen it before today, right?"

She glanced back in time to see Doreen and Ian exchanging a look. The Sinclairs and the too-handsome man all turned toward the display case.

Just as the glass exploded.

CHAPTER 5

$\mathcal{R}$iley dropped to the floor and covered her head with her arms. She swore she felt shards of glass whip over her and just knew she was going to end up with cuts all along her bare arms. The sound of the music box noise got louder, if anything, almost drowning out the sound of shattering glass and an entire display case full of music boxes collapsing into a heap.

A scream that had probably been her own echoed in all the noise. At least, she thought she might have screamed. It was hard to tell.

Next to her, she felt Ian and Doreen also hunkered on the ground. And the sound of that weirdly angry laughter filled the store, somehow easily heard even over all the chaos.

When she was sure no more glass was flying, she looked out through her arms. Then slowly sat up.

The case was a pile of glass and twisted metal and wooden boxes. A mess and a dangerous one with all the glass.

Doreen cursed. "How the hell do we get the Antashi box out of there now?"

She was right. Riley couldn't even see the box anymore.

Just piles of glass and metal and wood. The music boxes were still playing somehow, but were even noisier without the glass blocking some of the sound. And, though she couldn't be sure, it sounded like even more of the boxes were playing now.

At the top of the pile, Riley could just see the old box with the spinning ballerina on top. She was still spinning. But the movement was even more halting, happening in jolts and fits.

Poor box.

A whoosh of air, and suddenly Riley saw the pipes again, sitting on the top of the pile of glass.

That was…maybe not a good thing.

She looked up and back, to check on Doreen and Ian, and realized the too-handsome man was still standing. His hands held out in front of him, his palms facing the case. He hadn't ducked away from the exploding glass.

And he wasn't cut.

How?

She sat up fully, looking around her immediate area more closely. There was a circle of glass around her and the Sinclairs. A foot of space between them and a little line of piled, shimmering glass shards.

She blinked. Started to point out the circle. But Doreen and Ian climbed to their feet, Ian reaching an absent hand out to help Riley up. Most of his attention was on the pipes atop the pile of chaos that used to be a display case. So was Doreen's.

The too-handsome man lowered his arms and let out a huff. "That complicated things."

"You think," Doreen muttered.

"I'll go get the box," Ian said, straightening his vest. "But

I need you all to distract the fear dearg, or I'm not getting anywhere near the case."

"Anyone notice the circle of glass?" Riley asked, glancing around.

No one paid attention to her quietly spoken question. Honestly, she wasn't sure she'd spoken loud enough for them to hear anyway. There was still too much noise.

"How do we distract them?" Doreen asked the too-handsome man.

"Chase them."

"Chase them?"

"Chase them?" Riley squeaked. Like…run *toward* the mice or whatever the hell fear dearg were? That sounded like a bad idea. Especially with all the glass everywhere.

"Okay." Doreen pulled in a deep breath. "I'll go right. Riley, you go left. Circle around them. We should be able to scatter them." She looked at Ian. "You need anything?"

He pulled off his vest and wrapped it around one of his big hands. "I'm good. I'll need a minute, maybe two to find the box."

The too-handsome man motioned to Ian. "Give me your wrapped hand."

Ian held his hand out to the man, only half looking at him. Most of his attention on the shattered case.

The man took hold of Ian's vest-wrapped hand. A faint purple glow seemed to rise from between their clasped hands. The man's green eyes brightened briefly. And then he released Ian.

"That should help."

Ian glanced at his vest-wrapped hand. Shook his head. "Vest will never be the same."

"I'll buy you a new one," Doreen said. "Everyone ready?"

No, Riley thought. But she straightened her button-down

shirt and glanced to her left, looking for a path through the tables and display cases that would take her around and behind where the shattered case was.

Doreen bounced on her feet, her short-heeled boots squeaking against the wooden floor. That Riley could hear that squeak over the other noise sort of amazed her. And she realized a lot of the music box cacophony had died down. Now it was mostly just noise from the pipes and the angry laughter, and a few strained notes from a couple of boxes.

Doreen raised a hand.

Riley's heart hammered.

Doreen dropped her hand and shouted, "Now!"

Riley took off. Running along the path through the store she'd mapped out in her head, ducking when random things flew from shelves and racks. A plate crashing behind her. A folded jacket nearly hitting her in the face. A tin box clanked into an old-fashioned set of fire irons just as Riley passed.

Somewhere deep in her brain, she knew she wasn't chasing mice. Or even rats. Rats didn't throw things at you. But she couldn't make her eyes see clearly the creatures throwing things.

There were blurs of red flashing past. Here and there.

And one of those blurs did stop. Just long enough for her to swear a little man with pointed face and a tail, wearing a red suit and cap, stood on a shelf, his tail twitching at her. But the moment she blinked, the moment her brain tried to really *see* the little man…another blur of red. And her brain just saw a rat. That was all she could recall. The features of a rat.

She shivered and continued to race around the store. When she heard Doreen shouting, she started to shout and curse, too, making a lot of noise of her own. She snatched up a pot from a display of cookware and stared pounding the bottom of it to make more noise.

All the chaos she and Doreen were making seemed to anger the rat-things. Whatever they were. The laughter stopped. But the pipes continued to play and that music became so discordant, it actually hurt her ears.

She used the pot to knock away the various items thrown at her, faster and faster, and in between ducking and deflecting projectiles, pounded on the warn metal and shouted.

"Got it!" Ian yelled, his voice booming through the store.

"Herd them toward Ian," Doreen shouted.

Riley had no idea how to herd rats. She needed the pipes. The thought of becoming the Pied Piper nearly made her laugh, but she was too scared to laugh. She continued to pound on her pot, making noise and shouting, moving around toward the sound of Doreen's shouts and then angling back toward Ian.

She couldn't tell if this was having the desired effect or not. There were too many things being thrown at her. Too much noise and chaos. And she couldn't tell if it was coming from in front of her or from all around.

"Almost there," Doreen shouted.

Riley deflected a tossed rag doll, realized they'd made their way back into the toy section of the store, and looked up to see Ian standing on the other side of the shattered display case.

He held the wooden box with the inlaid Tree of Life on the lid.

CHAPTER 6

*R*iley had just enough time to recognize the box, just enough time to see Ian holding it, to see the too-handsome man standing a foot behind and to the right of Ian. A beat to knock away another random toy tossed at her head by the unseen menace racing around the store.

And then Doreen shouted, "Now!"

Ian opened the box.

The sound of screeching and shouting and cursing filled the air. And then a…cheer?

The race of air past. Streaks of red. They flew into the open box.

Riley caught the sight of one of those red blurs trying to crawl back out of the box, but Ian slammed the lid down.

"Do you have them all?" the too-handsome man asked.

"Think so. Doreen?"

"Think so." Doreen stepped out from behind a stack of old clocks.

Riley's brain screamed, *Think so?* But she kept her mouth shut.

Ian turned to face the too-handsome man. "Ready?"

The man held out something that looked like a large ring. Big enough to fit over two different fingers at once. But as she watched, the man twisted the ring. And twisted it again. And then again. Until the ring became a sphere. A sphere of gold. Gold that seemed to have a…

A purple shimmer?

The purple shimmer reminded her of the line of metal around the wooden pipes. The ring also seemed to have carvings on it. Swirls and knots. A pattern. A pattern she tried to make sense of but the image kept swimming away from her.

"I need the pipes," the too-handsome man said.

The pipes? Riley scanned the area. She hadn't seen it since circling back with Doreen, in the middle of all the chaos. Where had it landed?

"There!" In the middle of a pile of dolls. Again. And one of the dolls had rolled to look at Riley directly. Riley tried not to shiver as she hurried to retrieve the flute, reminding herself the dolls were just toys and there was nothing there looking out from those eyes.

She carried the instrument to the too-handsome man, giving Ian's box a wide birth. The lid was bouncing and there seemed to be shouting coming from inside. Did rats…curse like that? Maybe she was hearing the rats chittering, and it sounded weird because of the box.

After the man took the pipes from her, he motioned her back. "Stay behind me, please. Don't interfere."

Riley had no intention of interfering since she still wasn't sure what was happening.

The man set the pipes to his lips and started playing a song that was both melodious and a bit off. Not the discordant music that had been coming from the thing earlier when the…air currents had been causing it to make noise. But like the notes were one over. She didn't play an instrument. She wasn't sure what she meant by that thought. Just that it felt right.

And then, though she could still see the man playing the flute, his mouth running over the top of the different individual pipes, the sound disappeared. She could no longer hear it.

Was he still even playing or just pretending to play?

He lifted the sphere of golden rings in his palm higher. Gave Ian a slight nod. And Ian opened the box lid again.

Riley expected the blurs of red to come racing out again. To escape and rush into the rest of the shop, putting them right back to where they started. Instead, they seemed to float in the air in a cone of space, floating toward the sphere.

No resistance in the red blurs. They just rolled through the air toward the sphere.

Slowly enough Riley got another look that her brain couldn't quite turn into a reality. Little men-shaped creatures. Long faces. Noses that twitched. Long tails behind them. Short and round. But with red hats. Red suits. Red boots with curled toes on two feet. Men? Or rats? Or...something else?

What had Ian and Doreen called them? The fear dearg. The red men.

Her brain was still screaming that she was just seeing rats. That's all. A bunch of rats. And she was so horrified by all those rats, she was turning them into something less horrifying.

Like little men who looked a bit rat like and wore red suits.

She frowned. Not sure how her brain thought that was *less* horrifying.

The...whatever they were, flowed to the sphere of gold

rings and then popped inside it. With a strange sort of sucking sound, they disappeared, one by one, into the sphere.

The too-handsome man didn't stop playing the flute until the last of the blurs entered the sphere. Even though Riley still couldn't hear the music, it looked like the man's mouth worked across the pipes, and his cheeks puffed up as if he was blowing air into the pipes. She only got side views of him playing, because she was dutifully remaining behind him. But from her view, he still looked to be actively playing.

Once the last blur moved into the sphere, the man dropped the flute from his mouth, then set it absently onto a nearby table, his full attention on the sphere. He waved a hand over it, the purple glow brightened. So much, Riley narrowed her eyes. Finally had to close them.

A clap like thunder.

When Riley opened her eyes, the golden ring sat on the man's palm again. Just a ring. No sphere. There was still a series of knots and swirls around the gold. And a single glimmer of purple raced over the surface, then settled.

And it was just a ring.

CHAPTER 7

$\mathcal{R}$iley blinked and leaned in closer to the too-handsome man's back. The gold ring in his palm looked small enough now to fit onto a single finger instead of spanning two. Probably have to be her thumb to fit, but still. The piece had gone from something awkwardly sized, to something that looked like it belonged on a human finger.

The man slipped the ring onto his middle finger, then held up his hand to look at the ring closely. It fit perfectly. Looked just like a normal gold ring. Even winked with flashes of gold in the overhead light.

The man let out a long, slow breath.

Riley looked to her bosses. Doreen had sagged against the table with the clocks on it. Ian had closed the lid on the Tree of Life box and stood cradling it as he stared at the too-handsome man and his ring.

"They all in there?" Ian asked, breaking the silence.

And it was only then that Riley realized just how quiet it was now. No music. No crashing. No cursing. No tossed items. No chaos.

No noise.

One of the clocks on the table at Doreen's back ticked gently in the silent store, adding a rhythmic beat to Riley's shock.

"They're all in here," the man said. He finally looked away from the ring. "Thanks for your help." He glanced back at Riley, and for the first time smiled.

It was a stunning smile.

"Thank you, too," he said. "Good thing you'd spotted the Tree of Life box, huh?"

"Uh huh." Oh. That smile. She wasn't sure her brain was working anymore now. Actually, she was pretty sure her brain had stopped processing properly about twenty minutes ago. When she'd been worried about coming into the toy section to dust.

Dusting!

She looked around the store. It was an absolute mess. It would take them the rest of the afternoon and probably into tomorrow to get it straightened again. She sighed. Well, it was something to do.

The too-handsome man drew her attention again when he also sighed. "Sorry about the mess. Even sorrier I can't stay and help clean up. Have to get the ring back."

"Back where?" she asked, facing him again.

He glanced back at the Sinclairs. Doreen shrugged. Ian moved the box he still held under one arm and shrugged as well.

"Back to Faery," the man said, facing her again and smiling.

The smile caught her brain. She barely registered what he'd just said. "Faery, huh? Probably for the best. Suppose rats are less of a nuisance in Faery."

She had no idea what she was saying. Her thoughts were all swirling and her stomach was dancing and she was suddenly so aware of just how good looking the man was and how warm her clothes felt and how…restless she was.

The man's smile gentled. Then he glanced back at the Sinclairs. "I imagine the box and flute will stay here, but you might want to store the flute so it doesn't attract the little feckers again."

"We will," Ian said. He glanced down at the box. "You think it'll stay?"

"Probably. With the pipes here… Probably."

Ian nodded, looking like he was contemplating something. Then he retrieved the flute from where the man had left it. "I'll just get this into the storage room. You good, Dorrie?"

"Fine," she said with a slight smile and a wave to him. Doreen held a hand to her side, and her glasses were askew. She looked like she'd been in a fight, but had come out on the winning side.

But the way she was holding her side worried Riley. She hurried to Doreen, making an effort not to be obvious by brushing up against the too-handsome man. He did have to take a step back so she could pass, and his soft smile made her stomach dance again. Holy moly, was that a smile. He really should be on TV or in the movies.

She forced her brain to Doreen's possible injury. "You want to sit down?" she asked. "I can help you get to the back then start cleaning up. You look like you hurt something."

Doreen snorted. "One of the little bastards hit me with a ukulele right in the side. I didn't duck in time. That'll teach me, huh?" She chuckled. Then winced.

"You have a broken rib?" Ian asked, coming up to them.

"Don't think so, just a bruise. I'll take it easy." She gave Riley an apologetic look. "'Fraid that'll mean most of the store rearranging will be up to you and Ian. Sorry about that."

Riley waved that away. "Don't worry. We'll have it all back into shape in no time." She glanced at the too-handsome man from under her lashes, trying not to be obvious, but failing miserably.

"I'll get this into the storage room," Ian said, lifting the pipes a little. "Think we should leave the box in the front." He glanced back at the wrecked display case. "Once we get a new case." To Riley, he said, "Don't start working around the glass until I can help you. That's going to be delicate work."

"I'll start calling around to get us a new case since I can't help clean," Doreen said, trying to straighten fully and wincing. She cursed again. "Those little bastards aren't coming back now, are they? Now that they've managed to get in, does that make it easier for them to come back? We don't have a convenient cualthan around, and I haven't heard of a spare one coming up for trade."

"I'll see if I can find one for you," the too-handsome man said. "In the meantime, keep the pipes under lock and key, and they shouldn't be able to get in."

Riley found herself nodding and smiling stupidly at the man, not even the prospect of all the cleaning ahead of her dampening her fascination with him. "What's your name?" she asked without realizing she was going to.

He smiled at her. "I answer to a lot of names," he said.

Then proceeded to not give her a single one of them.

"Thanks again for your help," he said, lifting his hand with the ring on it. "Good luck." He tapped his fingers to his head in a little solute and sauntered out the door, into the bright afternoon sunlight.

Riley thought the sunlight paled in comparison to the man.

Doreen bumped her shoulder. "Don't let that one turn your head," she said. "It's more the glamour that's… interesting you. He's a real pain in the ass. Good guy. Just…a pain in the ass. And not what you might call human."

Riley blinked a few times and looked at Doreen. She must have heard that last sentence wrong. Not human? What was that supposed to mean?

"Come on," Doreen said, straightening her shoulders and only wincing a little. "Let's get started on all the cleanup. We should order in lunch today. I wouldn't mind pizza. How about you?"

"Pizza is good," Riley said. She glanced back at the door, where the too-handsome man had gone, and found herself wondering what he'd really looked like. Had he *really* been that handsome or was that just a trick of the stressful situation?

She helped Doreen to the back of the store and get settled at the counter, then got her a giant book with all her contact numbers in it from the office so she could start trying to locate a new display case. Riley wasn't entirely sure why she didn't just order one from a business supply store or something. She didn't understand the specifics of course. But she had worked a retail job where getting replacement display cases had been a matter of just…ordering one.

Doreen went about finding one like they had to have something specific and unique. Something that wasn't mass produced. When Riley asked, Doreen just said, "We need something special for those music boxes and that kind of case can be hard to find. I'll track something down."

The door behind the desk, the door that led into the back storage room opened and Ian walked out.

"Everything settled?" Doreen asked without look up from her book of contact numbers.

"All settled." Ian looked at Riley. "Ready to clean?"

"Sure."

"We're ordering pizza for lunch," Doreen said as she lifted the landline phone they kept under the counter.

Riley hadn't had access to a landline since she lived with her grandmother. She always found the fact that the siblings still had one quirky. It never rang. No one called the store on that line. It was just for calling out. Doreen had one in the office, too, but if she made calls in there, she usually had the door closed.

"Pizza is perfect." Ian pulled some brooms and dust pans out from a closet next to the storage room door. "Let's get started. We can make a fair job of getting all that glass up before the pizza arrives."

He handed Riley a pair of thick leather gloves, like construction worker's gloves. Which Riley took, bemused that he had these on hand. She supposed in an old store, glass things broke and had to be cleaned up.

As she moved back toward the toy section with Ian, she no longer felt that dread of going into the area as she had earlier. Probably because they'd managed to get rid of the rats. She really hated rodents. Some part of her brain must have just *known* they were back there.

Rats. Who played a reed pipe?

Yeah. Of course. That's what she'd seen get sucked into the…the rat trap thingy the handsome man had on him. Doreen must have called him in when they realized there were rats.

Part of her brain tried to remind her that the man had shown up before Doreen knew about the rats. But she must just be misremembering. Obviously, an exterminator had to be called in *after* they'd discovered the rats.

She set about carefully cleaning up the broken glass and twisted metal from the collapsed case, with Ian's help, moving the music boxes that had been inside the case carefully to a nearby table, shaking off the pieces of glass that stuck to them into the plastic garbage bin Ian had produced from somewhere. All the glass and metal went into the bin.

Lot of damage for a pack of rats. She didn't remember how the case had gotten shattered. Probably hit by some of the things flying off the shelves as the rats ran around. New York rats were nothing to mess with, that was for sure.

A flash of red hat and suit. The surly expression on a sharp little face. The angry angry laughter…

She must have just been imaging all that. Obviously, rats didn't laugh. Or wear red suits. If she thought about it, she should probably look up the species of rat. The others had called them something specific. If she ever remembered those words again, she'd look them up.

But for now, they had a store to clean. And pizza on the way. And thankfully, no more infestations to worry about for now.

And best of all, she hadn't had to go in the back storage room this time.

(*This time?*)

She'd only been back there once or twice and was happy not to go again. The place was a little dark.

(*Dark? More like scary. More like weird.*)

"Pizza will be here in fifteen," Doreen called from the back of the store.

Riley's stomach growled and Ian chuckled. "Even fighting a pest infestation didn't dampen your appetite, eh?"

"Now that the pests are gone, I'm good," she said.

She frowned as she looked around the toy section, trying to remember what seemed to be missing. There'd been a box out here, hadn't there? One she really liked. Something with a tree on it

Ah well. They must have sold it on one of her days off.

Riley turned her attention back to the cleanup, anticipating pizza, and enjoying the rhythmic routine of tidying up the store.

SINGS THE FOREST

I was a forest nymph. Once. A long time ago, when humans were in their infancy. I was small and brown, and I ran through the woods, a breeze on the forest floor. The ground moved well beneath my feet.

We lived alone then, gathering once in a while for a party or a talk. But mostly, we lived alone.

My specialty was the pine.

I could climb higher than most, not as high as some. We were earth creatures. No wings. No flight.

I never met a fairy. I don't think they're real.

I loved stories. I could climb a pine tree and listen to the leaves' story for hours. The birds would help; they added the music. They were air creatures.

When the rains came, we danced. Lightning flashes and thunder claps kept the beat and rhythm. I was good at the dance. Streams swelled. The mud choked our feet, squished through our toes. The forest dripped for a long time after the rains. Then the dance stopped.

I don't remember what I ate. If I ate. It didn't matter. The trees mattered.

She was born to a good mother, the little doe with the spotted backside. She was my friend. So too her daughter, and her daughter's daughter. They were all good mothers.

When winter came, we slept. I burrowed beneath my pine tree, and she kept me warm. She was a good mother, too.

I saw the hut for the first time when I was old. There were more when I saw it again.

I died when lightning struck my tree. Of a tree I was born. So too for a tree I did die. She lived a long time.

I was a forest nymph. Once.

BLACK WATER HAWTHORNS

CHAPTER 1

alking through the University College Dublin campus this late at night wasn't a normal part of Dierdre's routine.

Her normal routine involved being off campus by dinner time, taking the long walk from the Belfield campus back to the room she rented in a terraced house in Dun Laoghaire so there were no phones for her supervisor or any of the people in her lab to reach her for a good solid hour and a half, and trying not to stress out about the fact that she had only one more month to finish her thesis or she'd have to take out more student loans.

She did not want to deepen the dept she was already in for her Ph.D. If she could get the thesis turned in before the end of next month, she wouldn't need to register for the new academic year, which meant she wouldn't need to take out another loan. She'd be broke, but she'd minimize her debt.

And all that depended on getting this thesis done in a month.

Except things weren't going well.

Which meant she found herself staying later and later into

the night. Pushing till she had to leave or risk missing the last bus home. She was fine walking all the way to Dun Laoghaire when it was still light out. Even twilight wasn't too bad because she got through the dodgier part of her walk earlier on. And the sun set this time of year wasn't until after seven thirty. But after that, every route home passed through sections of housing estates that were too dark for a woman walking alone at night.

Not that she usually had much trouble in Dublin. The Irish men seemed to be a little afraid of her when she opened her mouth and her still-very-American accent came out. Something about Americans and guns, apparently. Still, she didn't like to take chances.

Tonight, she'd really pushed the limits, though. She might find herself walking home yet. Or maybe sleeping in the lab. No late-night buses would be running on a random Wednesday. And the last DART train—still a walk through an area that was too quiet and dark now—left in an hour. She wasn't going to be ready to leave in an hour.

Staying on campus this late made her jittery, though.

Especially given the recent gossip circulating among the postgrads about people just disappearing off campus.

Not that there was proof or evidence of real disappearances. No one outside the campus even seemed to be talking about it. That one undergrad who'd supposedly gone missing last week? No missing persons report had been filed with the Guardi. The librarian's assistant who went for coffee four nights ago and never came back? Apparently, she and her boss had had a fight and she'd just quit. And that visiting lecturer in the history department who'd missed a lecture night before last? Dierdre's friend doing a post-doc in history said he had some family problems and had probably just flown back to Scotland without giving notice.

All very reasonable explanations for why people might not be where they were expected. Lots of people on campus were on edge, though. But she wrote that off to academic deadlines. It was that time of year. She wasn't the only one staying too late and living off coffee.

Speaking of coffee.

Faint lights cast dancing shadows along the path next to the library as she made her way to the student center and the still-open donut shop. Her need for coffee and sugar overwhelming at this stage, she was grateful the place recognized its importance to campus life and didn't close early.

Out of habit, she glanced toward the pond that took up the center of campus. No ducks or birds seemed to be in the dark expanse of water. Not even anything sleeping that she could see. Though the area around the large, artificial, figure eight pond was pretty dark.

Nearer the buildings, the shadows were pushed back by bright light spilling out of the library. She wasn't the only student pushing deadlines and burning the candle late to get work done. Despite that sign of life, though, the campus was otherwise very quiet. Most of the undergrads had left hours ago. There were no dorms or student housing on the campus. And unless they had deadlines of their own, all the lecturers had gone home by tea-time.

Mostly just postgrads at this stage. And none of them were wandering around the darkened campus at the moment.

Usually, Dierdre liked the silence and quiet. She preferred being alone when she had to think. But tonight, with missing persons gossip in the back of her mind, the silence was almost eerie.

She paused, scanning her surroundings again. Tall buildings encircled the pond, quiet and dark. The faint noises of the city distant and indistinct. A gentle breeze blew through the trees beside the pond, carrying a faint whiff of stale mustiness and bird poop from the dark water. Underneath that, the siren call of over-brewed coffee.

She shook herself out of her revere. No danger here. Just the promise of coffee. Bad coffee, but still. She didn't need good coffee right now. Gut burning sludge would do so long as it had caffeine and kept her awake another hour or two.

The student center was just past the library, and under a dark overhang that cut off the glow coming from the other building. In that darkness, with only the bright pink light ahead to the donut shop to guide her, Deirdre felt momentarily like she was in a different world.

And well, technically, she was. Ireland was a long way from her home in San Diego, California. But different as Ireland was from home, it was still just an ordinary place. With ordinary people doing ordinary things like working and singing and drinking and fighting and loving and…all the things she wasn't doing while desperately trying to finish her thesis.

She sighed and took a step toward the salvation of coffee. Only to pull up short…

As the world folded and stretched around her.

Bulging and tightening like a breath.

The darkness pulled and lengthened, making it seem as if the lights from the donut shop were miles away instead of a few yards. The air felt denser and thicker. Colder than the early spring normally got, even this late at night. Like someone had opened a freezer at her back.

Her ears popped, and her head felt fuzzy, stuffed full of cotton.

For a terrifying instant, she thought she might pass out.

Woah. This was bad. Bad bad bad.

She'd pushed too hard. Her body was rebelling. Too much coffee and sugar, not enough fruits and vegetables, too much stress and not enough sleep. And worse, no one around to find her if she did pass out. No telling how long it would take for the campus security to drive past this area in their little golf cart.

The world settled, the temperature returned to a balmier spring coolness, the weird stretching of shadows receded until the brightly lit shop ahead looked a normal distance away.

Deirdre blinked hard a few times, and shook her head. The dizziness faded. The blackness that had edged her vision pulled back.

Okay. Warning received. No more coffee. No more sugar. She was done for the night. She would go home and have her panic attack there where it was safe and her roommates would take care of her if she did pass out in the sitting room.

She turned to head back toward the lab, the faint orange sidewalk lights breaking up the darkness enough…

To make the glowing white stag standing a few feet away impossible to miss.

CHAPTER 2

$\mathcal{D}$ierdre wondered if she really had passed out. Because this had to be a dream.

The stag was huge. Easily the size of one of the now-extinct Giant Irish Red deer. Ten, twelve feet tall, crowned with an impressive rack of antlers that spread out wide and resembled nothing less than tree branches sporting clumps of dirt and grass. The animal's white fur glowed, lit from within. So bright it was difficult to look at.

But more terrifying than the giant antlers and glowing fur... The beast's eyes were red.

Not just red rimmed around ordinary brown eyes. No. Red all the way through. With a very faint black pupil in the center.

She had to be dreaming. This wasn't the sort of creature that existed in reality.

The stag pawed the stone walkway, the sound like metal hitting metal, throwing up sparks. The stag glanced toward the pond, and despite herself, Dierdre followed the creature's gaze.

Gasping, she fell back a step, coming up hard against one

of the steel columns supporting the overhand in front of the student center.

The pond was no longer an artificial figure-eight of water, surrounded by small bushes, manicured grass, and a handful of oak trees. Now giant oaks with branches as thick as her torso stretched over a natural body of lapping water.

Black water. That had sparkles of light dancing across the surface.

Rocks and rough grass along the banks replaced the border of small stones and wooden walkway with its stone benches. Thick vines and impenetrable brambles filled in the undergrowth going all the way to the edge of the black pond. Instead of the slightly stale smell of recirculated water and bird poop, now all Dierdre could smell was fresh, rain-soaked air, a thick loamy earth scent. And just a hint of…sulfur?

She pressed harder against the steel at her back and rubbed her eyes. This wasn't…wasn't possible. She'd pushed her body too hard. Her mind. Something had obviously broken inside her. She was hallucinating. Unconscious.

She actually glanced back at the spot where she'd been standing when her surroundings had seemed to fold and contract around her, expecting to see her unconscious body on the walkway.

But no. Nothing there. The lights from the library were still behind her. In the distance, she could just hear a surge of traffic over the motorway. But the trees and brambles rose so high in front of her, they blocked the white stone and glass façade of O'Reilly Hall beyond.

Behind her, the campus she knew. In front of her…

Something else altogether.

This definitely had to be a dream.

The stag stomped the stone walkway again, more sparks flew in Dierdre's peripheral vision. From the depths of the black water, something luminous and pale rose. She stumbled closer for a better look.

A dancing ball of soft purplish-blue light with a bright white star spark in the center.

She glanced at the stag, still standing where she'd left it.

"What's this?" she asked. The sound of her voice reverberated strangely in the air. The fact that she was speaking to a *deer* probably would have surprised her more if she wasn't convinced she was hallucinating.

The stag whinnied, then snorted. Steam streamed from its nose. When the stag opened its mouth, fire filled the animal's insides, a hollow furnace of red and orange.

It moved toward her, until all she could see was the flaming tunnel inside its mouth. She stumbled backward, away from the beast, away from that hell's gate.

And tripped into the shallows of the black pond.

Deirdre barely had a chance to register the water seeping into her hiking boots, sealing her cargo pants to her calves, when something grabbed her ankle.

She looked down, had a moment to gasp.

Before she was dragged beneath the surface.

From the edge of the water, the stag watched the surface settle, the last bubble of protest rise and pop. In the center of the lake, the fairy light winked. The stag shook his head, tufts of the grass and soil decorating his antlers dropping into the black water, breaking the surface.

He moved toward the brambles under a big oak, settling into the underbrush to wait.

CHAPTER 3

*D*eirdre gasped, sucking in water, choking. The blackness closed around her. Something sharp pierced her ankle, through the thick side of her boot, pain ripping up her leg.

She swung her arms desperately upward, grasping for the surface, struggling to break free. Nothing but water around her. She wasn't even sure if she was pointing up or down anymore. The tug on her ankle went one way and she fought to go the opposite.

Though she couldn't see, she could feel her mind going black, her lungs on fire, unconsciousness pulling her under.

But wasn't she dreaming? Wasn't this a hallucination?

It felt like death.

She grasped at the surrounding water, reaching for something, anything. Some purchase. Some lifeline she could use to pull herself to the surface, to breathable air.

A glimmer of light above her. She reached for it. Closed her hand. Felt only water.

Abruptly, the hold on her ankle vanished, and she popped up to the surface like a cork. She choked as she tried to pull in air, could feel the cool breeze on her cheeks, but all she got was another swallow of water, more choking. Darkness covering her vision.

Arms flailing, she caught something thick and solid overhead and clung to it. The solid object gave her enough purchase to clear her lungs, cough up the water, pull in desperately needed oxygen.

Several moments passed, long deep breaths, her throat and lungs burning from the abuse. When she felt like she could breathe again, felt like she wasn't going to drown, she looked around. The library was still brightly lit just beyond the thick stand of oaks and brambles. But she was deep inside the pond now. Out near the middle of it.

And the strange forest that had grown up around it had thickened. She wasn't sure how to get back to the library and student center from where she was. How to even get up onto the shore. The underbrush came all the way to the edge of the water. The oak branches crossed, their thick trunks and roots so tightly packed, she couldn't see a path through.

But she had to get out of the water. Something was in this pond. Something that had tried to drown her.

She looked up and finally realized she was grasping a tree branch stretched out over the water. And she was closer to an edge than she realized. Still not much of a shoreline. But a small half circle of flat grass would at least give her a place to get out.

What the hell had grabbed her?

Her ankle still hurt like hell, but she couldn't tell if she was bleeding or not.

She struggled to the shore, keeping a hand on the oak branch. She had the vague thought that if whatever was beneath the surface grabbed her again, she could pull herself up onto the branch. The branch was certainly thick enough to hold her. Her inability to do a pull up was the flaw in the plan.

She made the edge of the pond and scrambled onto the soft grass on her hands and knees. The relief of being out of the black water had her shaky and doubled over as she tried to slow her heartbeat, tried to drag in steadying breaths.

When she lifted her head, the stag stood a few feet away, surrounded by ferns and oak. And right next to him, a hawthorn tree. There weren't any hawthorn trees on campus, last she checked.

She glanced away long enough to verify she could still see the library building. A part of her knew if she could just get back there, back to those artificial lights and other human beings, she'd be okay.

But the building looked very far away.

Deirdre faced the stag again. It snorted and nodded to the grass.

Frowning she looked down and realized she was grasping something in one hand, something she hadn't even noticed.

A key.

It was long, and silver, an old-fashioned style with a heart-shaped head and a prong at the end with cuts that would open the lock. The silver surface showed a faint purple shimmer before settling into ordinary metal.

"What's this?" she asked the stag.

It snorted, shook its head, and turned into the undergrowth.

Somewhere in the back of her mind, distant with time, a voice told her that she shouldn't follow that stag. Something remembered from a fairytale.

Still, she found herself standing on trembling legs. Walking into the undergrowth. Pushing aside low limbs, ducking under thick branches, tripping over stretched roots.

Following the stag.

An image of the furnace inside its mouth made her stumble and glance back over her shoulder. She could no longer see the library through the forest. Just the pond, the water black and still.

She stumbled forward another few steps and her ankle screamed at her. Damn it, she'd forgotten all about that. Though how, she wasn't sure.

A quick glance confirmed a hole in her thick boot. Whatever had pierced that leather had been strong. Now that she wasn't in the water, though she was soaked to the bone, she'd swear she could feel blood dripping down her foot, settling under her heel.

She stopped to investigate, but ahead of her, the stag made a chuffing noise and pawed the ground, barking at her in a noise that reminded her of a seal.

"Can't stop, huh?" she muttered. "If I bleed to death, it's your fault."

Not that she thought the stag cared. And really, she was more worried about whatever poison or bacteria might be seeping through her blood than bleeding out from the puncture wound.

The stag turned and moved deeper into the trees again. Despite herself, Deirdre continued to follow.

This part of the woods went on farther than it should have if the ordinary physical layout of the campus were the limits. They should be coming up to the back of the science center, the east wing where the chemists hung out. Her lab was in the biology wing on the opposite side of the building. Still, she'd take the chemistry wing. She'd take anything familiar in that moment.

Yet all she saw ahead was the stag's retreating flank and more forest.

As she passed her sixth hawthorn tree, it struck her that the stag seemed to be following a path of hawthorns. Individual trees strung out like pearls through the forest. For some reason, that made her feel less lost. If she turned around, she could follow the hawthorns back to the pond, back to a place where she could see the library. Where it was obvious they were still on campus.

She glanced over her shoulder, confirming the hawthorns were still behind her. And took a steadying breath.

Her ankle hurt like hell. Her lungs burned. Her throat was raw. The key in her hand felt heavier than it should. She was soaked to the skin, her cargo pants clinging to her legs, her fleece zip up stretched out of shape and rubbing weirdly against her arms. She was starting to shiver even though the air felt remarkably balmy and warm.

Yes, actually. Quite warm. Warmer than it had been when she'd gone into the water.

Too warm for this time of year.

She tripped over a branch, grunted a curse, and looked over her shoulder again.

The undergrowth behind her shivered. A vibration bounced up through her feet. Ferns parted and fell back toward each other again.

Something growled.

Deirdre's heartbeat sped as terror and another jolt of adrenaline shot through her.

Wet clothes forgotten, she rushed forward, stumbling over roots, attempting to run on an ankle that kept trying to fold over. Pain screamed up her leg, but she ignored it.

Because the growl was getting closer.

She closed the distance between herself and the stag. Or at least she tried to. But every time she swore she was closer to the beast, she'd blink and it would be as far ahead as it had been moments before.

Branches grabbed at her soaked clothes. Pulling. Ripping. A sting on her cheek. Small cuts along her hands.

The growl behind her nearing.

Panting, desperate, she forced her way through undergrowth that seemed to be thickening, seemed to be *trying* to stop her.

The stag's white glow got fainter ahead. Panic tore through Deirdre until she was shaking as she ran, forcing her way past grasping branches and thorn-thick vines. What happened if she lost sight of the stag?

Or had the stag led her into a trap?

The growl neared.

She screeched between her teeth, afraid to scream. Afraid if she didn't scream, she'd burst. The part of her that studied animal behavior thought running away from the thing behind her might be spurring it on. But that did nothing to slow down the pure, unadulterated animal panic that sent her desperately forward.

She could almost feel hot breath against the back of her neck. The hair on her body rose. She could barely breathe. She was going to hyperventilate.

Risking a single glance back, all she could see was moving underbrush, getting closer, moving fast. That growl shivering through the air.

Deirdre squeaked and pushed harder through the brush until she rammed tight into a thicket of brambles, the sharp thorns tearing into her clothes, drawing blood, scrapping her up until she could feel that blood dripping over her skin. The brambles closed around her, trapping her.

She couldn't move.

The scream clawed at her throat, poised to escape.

She faced her pursuer.

A huge, dark shadow rose out of the underbrush.

DEEP IN THE WOODS, IN THE DARKNESS UNDER THICK OAK branches, a fairy light danced, lighting the last hawthorn tree. The stag pawed the ground at the base of the tree and snorted. Steam from his nostrils puffed over the lock.

The stag shook his head and some of the grass and dirt in his antlers filtered to the ground, a brief, earth-scented rain.

In the distance, he heard the woman scream. Heard the growl.

The Dobhar-Chú had found her.

CHAPTER 4

From the rustling ferns, a creature of darkness rose. Nothing but shadows under the tree overhangs. Though Dierdre couldn't see the being clearly, it was easily ten feet tall, its head brushing the high oak branches. The body was thick, the head large and obscured by shadow. But when it opened its mouth, like the stag, the inside was a red and orange seething cauldron of flame and heat.

The creature made a noise like a high-pitched chittering screech.

And Dierdre screamed.

She struggled against the brambles holding her in their solid grasp, tearing skin and clothes without thought. Whatever that thing was, it dropped down and landed close enough for her to smell the murky pondwater stench of it.

The thing that had dragged her under. The thing that had something sharp enough to pierce leather.

If that sharp part of its body could easily run through her boot, it could also easily run through her flesh.

She screamed again when she felt the heat of its breath. Too close. Getting closer.

With a mighty tug born of complete and utter panic, she jerked and stomped and tore her way free of the bramble patch, losing a sleeve to the needle-sharp thorns as she did. She didn't care. The moment she popped free of the tangle she tore off in the direction the stag had gone. At least, she thought she was running in the right direction. It was so dark under the trees, so utterly black. As black as the water had been.

But there…a faint glowing light.

And another hawthorn tree!

She raced to the tree, then past, running toward the faint glow beyond.

A part of her, a small part that was still rational, wondered why she was racing toward the stag. The stag had gotten her into this mess. The stag might have been the one to lay a trap for her. To feed her to whatever was following her.

She should be racing back toward the library, toward the light and the human beings she knew were behind her somewhere.

But the creature with the terrifying growl and the scent of pond water surrounding it was also back that way.

Her lizard brain was too panicked for any other thought than to run *away* from the thing chasing her. And to head for the only source of light.

She skidded to a stop when she burst through more undergrowth and landed in a small clearing.

Circled by oaks, carpeted in soft, spongy grass. Little sparks of light danced around the clearing, like fireflies. And at one end, the stag stood, glowing white in the darkness.

Beside the stag, under a ball of light like the one that had been in the center of the lake, was another hawthorn tree.

This hawthorn's thorny branches were exposed, no leaves or flowers blooming. Only a silvery bark and two-inch-long spikes lining its skinny limbs. And in the center of the narrow trunk, was a tall, thin...

Door.

Or maybe just a rectangular cut in the tree. Maybe just that. Because if she turned a little and looked at the cuts from the corner of her eye, the hawthorn just looked like a normal tree, its bark lined and rough, with tiny shadows in the crevices that could, if looked at just right, maybe be a...

Door.

The stag stomped the ground and snorted, steam rushing across the hawthorn's trunk, like fog filling the clearing. She looked down and realize there was a fog rising. She could no longer see her feet.

Behind her, the sound of the creature that had been chasing her crashing through the underbrush.

She looked between the stag and the tree, then toward the noise of the approaching pond creature.

The stag stomped the earth again, sending up sparks.

Deirdre jumped. And for reasons she couldn't explain to herself, she moved closer to the steam-snorting stag, closer to the hawthorn tree with its weirdly cut bark that sort of looked like a door.

When she was right in front of the tree, she finally spotted something small and silver, at the edge of the cuts that resembled a door.

A lock.

A silver panel with a keyhole in the center. The panel bore elaborate Celtic knot designs raised from the metal, winding around the central keyhole in a way that made the keyhole look like an eye.

The keyhole itself was the old-fashioned kind, with a

circle on top and a small straight section beneath. Old fashioned... Just like the key from the pond.

The key she, miraculously, still held.

"I'm supposed to open the lock?" she asked the stag.

It snorted and stomped the ground.

"What am I releasing?"

Not that the stag could answer that question. Would it, even if it could?

Behind her, the low growl of the pond creature.

Okay. She had two choices. Run away and not do as the stag asked, but risk confronting the monster behind her again, or worse, getting lost in this strange forest and never getting out. She could try to run back along the hawthorn path to safety and humanity—if she could find those things.

Or she could see what all this was about and open the lock.

Her panicking lizard brain could think of nothing but running. Running fast and far. Getting away. But a part of her recognized that would be futile. There was nowhere to run to. No chance of getting far enough away.

She looked at the key. Looked at the hawthorn.

And raised the key to the lock.

A screech of protest behind Deirdre, just as her key touched the lock panel. Something large crashed into the clearing. Her back hunched, ready for a strike, a blow, terrified of the death looming over her, casting shadows across the hawthorn, shadows that wavered in the little glowing ball of light over her head.

The stag stomped a hooved-foot again, striking more sparks.

Deirdre ignored her panic and the screaming demand of her body to run, and slid the old-fashioned key into the keyhole surrounded by elaborate Celtic knots.

Another whine of protest behind her, a sound almost like a dog but with something like a seal's bark underneath. A sound that reminded her a little of the barking sound the stag had made at her before she stepped close to the pond and got dragged under.

Had that even been the stag? Or had she been hearing this creature?

Or was she just losing her mind?

She took a deep breath, closed her eyes, and turned the key.

The key jerked out of her hand.

Panicked, she opened her eyes. The lock panel seemed to have retreated. The hawthorn farther away than it had been a moment before. That sense of the space around her stretching, lengthening, distorting. Just like under the overhang outside the student center.

She reached toward the key where it was still firmly inside the lock. Far away now. Too far to grasp.

A cracking noise filled the clearing, pierced the wooly sensation in her head, stuffing her ears.

Another growl. A whine.

And then a burst of light, so bright and white and powerful, Deirdre raised her arm to cover her eyes, sure the light would slam into her like a blow.

*D*ierdre fell. Not just fell. Was falling. Falling. Farther than just to the ground. Too long to have just been knocked onto the grass. Like she'd stepped back into a deep well and was in freefall, the hard ground very far below.

When she did hit solid earth, she grunted and her breath rushed out of her. She couldn't utter a sound, not even a scream.

For a long moment, she just laid where she was, certain she'd fallen to her death.

Slowly, she realized she could feel spongy grass beneath her back. Smell earth and a hint of rain in the air. She blinked open her eyes. Stars winked down at her. In the distance, clouds rolled across the sky. Clouds made slightly orange from the city lights beneath them.

City lights.

Dublin.

She sat up abruptly, groaning when a pain sliced through her head. But her body wasn't broken. In fact, outside of a sort of worked-out-too-hard soreness, she felt fine.

She glanced down at her boot, at the place where... something had pierced her ankle. The hole was obvious in the leather. But when she removed the shoe, her ankle looked fine. No sign of the puncture wound she'd been sure was there. Her leg didn't hurt anymore either.

Slowly, it sank in that she wasn't wet anymore either. Her clothes were torn but dry. And where she'd thought she'd lost an entire sleeve of her fleece, it turned out there was just a jagged hole in it, nothing worse.

Sucking in a slow breath, she looked around. Across the pond, the lights of the library and student center looked so ordinary, Dierdre had to blink a few times.

She glanced around and realized she was on the grassy hill outside the white stone O'Reilly Hall. In a completely different place than she'd thought she'd been when inside the thick oak forest.

There was no sign of the oak forest anymore, either. And the pond looked as it always did, an artificial figure eight, its banks made up of small, stacked stones. The grass, the small wooden walkway near the library side, the occasional stone bench...

All very normal.

Using the gentle downward slope of the hill, she pushed herself up fully into a sitting position. And finally noticed she wasn't alone. Next to her, three other people. Two women and a man. All curled up on their sides, like they were asleep. None of them looked familiar.

She shook one of the women gently. She was dressed in a long black skirt and a loose white jumper, one of the pretty Irish wool corded sweaters Deirdre had started collecting whenever she had a few spare quid. The stranger blinked her eyes open, and sat up abruptly. Looking around frantically as she pushed her shoulder-length brown hair off her face.

"Where am I? Still inside? Is this—" She cut herself off abruptly when she spotted the library.

And then she started to cry.

Wordlessly, and a little panicky, Dierdre pulled the stranger to her, hugging her close.

"I thought I'd never get out," the woman sobbed. "I thought I'd be trapped there forever."

Her Irish accent was soft and clipped. Dierdre thought maybe it was a Dublin accent but after nearly four years, she still wasn't great with picking out the different regional accents. She could usually tell when someone was from Cork, but that was about it.

"What's your name?" Dierdre asked, softly.

"Fiona," the woman said.

TURNED OUT FIONA WAS THE MISSING LIBRARIAN'S assistant. The man was the missing lecturer from Scotland. The other woman was the undergrad who'd been missing for a week.

None of them remembered much. Images of a white stag. Of a deep black-water pond. Of something sharp piercing their skin. Of a huge creature that resembled a strange cross between a giant dog and an otter, with sharp teeth and claws like daggers.

And then of being trapped in a glittering clearing in the middle of a forest, with trees that didn't look like anything they'd seen before and a sky that never darkened. None of them could say how long they'd been inside that strange world, except to say that it had felt like a long time.

Deirdre tried to gently explain how they'd been noticed missing, at least on campus. That it had only been a week for the undergrad, less time for the others. But their disorientation and confusion took another hour to sort out.

In the end, they all hurried past the pond to the still open donut shop, to the light and the burnt coffee and the sweet donuts and the sense of reality.

Like the others, Dierdre wasn't sure she'd ever be able to walk next to the pond again without rushing past. Without seeing the strange oak forest and the dark, black waters.

But the stress and overwhelm of getting her thesis finished had, at least momentarily, abated. She was exhausted. But she was alive. So were the others. Whatever it was they'd lived through—and they might not ever fully understand it—but whatever had happened, it was done now.

Back to the Ireland she knew. The ordinary place, with ordinary people, doing ordinary things like working and singing and drinking and fighting and loving…all the things she wasn't doing as she finished her thesis.

Where fairytales were just made-up stories to amuse tourists, and no one actually believed Faery was real or that hawthorn trees were gateways into that other world.

And where four people who may, or may not, have been dragged into Faery, decided over stale coffee and sugary donuts that whatever they'd experienced, it must have been a dream. A collective delusion brought on by stress and working too hard.

Everyone was fine now. Everything was good. And normal.

No need to pay attention to that glowing white stag, standing just outside their peripheral vision at the edge of the pond. Tomorrow, they'd be back to work, back to all the ordinary things.

Tonight…

Tonight, they'd stick to the artificial lights of the human world.

And share a taxi home.

THE FAIRIES AND THE
BRIER

Shall I tell you, then, about the Good People of Bennettsbridge, in county Kilkenny, near the river Nore, who I have never met myself (for they hide whenever I come around, being a storyteller as I am, and they being so jealous of what's said about them—and they knowing I tell what stories come to me), but I've had the tale from one who knows the one who saw it happen.

Now as you know, the Good People are as often troublesome as they are helpful. And they do as the whim takes them, giving not a fig for the end results. But every now and then the end is all to the good.

It just so happened then, that living in Bennettsbridge, near the river Nore, was a young man whose parents, God bless them, had passed away, leaving the lad a small patch of farmland and a few head of sheep. Dohmnall, as the young man was known, lived not grand but well enough off the bit of land and, doing so in such an honest way, was generally regarded as a decent man.

There also lived in this same village a man most knew only as the Brier. And he, afflicted with greed and gluttony worse than most, took it into his head to own Dohmnall's small patch of land, though why no one can say. But rich though he was, the Brier could not buy the land from Dohmnall, who would not sell no matter the offer, for 'twas his father's land.

Then the Brier, greedy devil that he was, turned to the law. But the constable would not be bought against young Dohmnall, nor the judge neither. This all left the Brier without recourse save one. If Dohmnall would not sell so long as the land could support him, then the Brier would see the land ruined for the season.

With these, the devil's own plans, made, the Brier

sneaked up on Dohmnall's land late one moonless night. He first led away the few head of sheep to a spot along the river where the drop was steep, and over the edge he sent them to their deaths. Next, to Dohmnall's crops he sprinkled a withering potion (for 'tis said the Brier's grandmother was a witch of the most evil sort, who taught him a trick or two of the black arts) and watched with his own eyes as the new plants blackened and shrunk back into the ground.

All this the Brier would have got away with, for he had fashioned to put blame on the fairies for Dohmnall's troubles, but the Good People discovered the plot.

Now they, caring little for the mischief humans do each other as they are not but mischief makers themselves, would have left the Brier be had he not tried to put the blame to them. As I said before, they are a jealous lot, wanting none to take credit for their own deeds, but also not wanting the blame for deeds done by others.

So on that same moonless night, as the Brier slunk away to his own house, the Good People went to work on Dohmnall's land.

Next morning when the young man rose, what should he see but his crop come full season and ready for harvesting in one night, and his sheep, now double in number, all sheered, their wool piled in bundles by his door. Dohmnall, being not the kind to question, harvested his crop, and after selling both it and the wool, had enough profit to live as he did for the next year.

Of course and we all know that the Brier, having witnessed the selling, was none too happy, knowing that Dohmnall must be up to mischief. Thinking so, he went again in the darkest hours of night to Dohmnall's land, and once again, he drove the sheep into the river and poisoned the soil of the field.

Next morning Dohmnall awoke to a new crop, ready to harvest, and freshly sheered sheep, double again what they had been the previous day, their wool piled in bundles at the young man's door.

As he'd not replanted the day before, and as he knew the sheep had been sheered just the day before, Dohmnall suspected the Good People were about some strange business, the reasons for which only they and God could know. But he reckoned, and rightly so, that if the Good People wanted to sheer his sheep and plant his crops, then 'twas no business of his. Once again, he sold the wool and new harvested crops and took home enough money for another year of living as he did.

For three weeks, the People played their game with the Brier and for all of those three weeks, Dohmnall's wealth grew. So many sheep did he by then possess, that he bought a larger bit of land to add to his own. And before too long, Dohmnall had risen to be one of the wealthiest men in all of county Kilkenny. He continued to deal fairly and honest with all those around him, and never did he let a day pass when he did not thank the Good People with a pitcher of milk on his window sill. And Dohmnall has lived a wealthy and happy man from that day to this.

As for the Brier, he is said to have wandered too close to a fairy fort at the last day of the third week of his war with the Good People, and none, to my knowledge, have heard a word of him since.

TO DANCE IN FALLOW
FIELDS AT MIDNIGHT

CHAPTER 1

*B*ecks walked past the pond down the lane from her house, the sun soft on her skin as the birds and bugs droned in the early autumn warmth. She'd been struggling with her novel for hours and needed out of the house, needed to go for a walk. And the day had turned out beautiful.

If only she could better enjoy it.

Her head spun and whirled and frustration gnawed at her. Deadlines loomed. A problem with a galley proof came up last minute. And her current novel was so stuck she wanted to chuck the whole thing into the pond.

She'd indulged an old dream coming here. Renting a cottage in Ireland. Mostly to write. A little bit to escape. But mostly to write. Unfortunately, the dream was slowly turning into a nightmare. All the usual problems and issues followed her here. The writing wasn't an uninterrupted free for all as she'd hoped. And she'd been sleeping bad for the last week thanks to some strange sounds coming from the direction of the pond. She thought it might be someone's escaped herd of sheep. But when she went down to the pond in the morning after the second night, she hadn't seen anything that looked like sheep hoof prints.

She'd come down to the pond every morning for a week after the noise and bad night's sleep. Whatever the ruckus was, there was no evidence of it in the morning. That didn't help her sleep.

The dirt path to the pond was bracketed by grass as green as you might expect in Ireland. And the area was dotted with trees, she thought oaks but needed to look them up. The pond itself was just a small hole in the ground, barely three feet across. She could probably jump over it if she got a running start.

Beyond the pond was a stacked stone fence, broken by a metal swing gate over a metal cattleguard. She was a city girl, she'd never seen a cattleguard before and had had to ask one of the locals at the pub what the metal grate was for. The one thing about this dream trip turning nightmare that *had* worked out as she'd hoped was the cozy local pub with lots of Irish music and beer and, as the Irish said, craic. Fun. She loved that word for fun. And the locals hadn't chuckled too long at her not knowing what a cattleguard was.

Her one superpower was being able to ask questions without worrying that they were stupid questions. In her heart of hearts, she knew every question, no matter how ridiculous, was valid. And that attitude almost always got her answers supplied generously. Once the answerer accepted that she was sincere in her question.

The fields beyond the metal gate and cattleguard seemed to be fallow. There was only dark, rich soil, green green grass, and a lot of rocks. At the far side, a little stream surrounded by trees was just visible. She'd been tempted to go down to the stream since first arriving. But when she set a hand on the gate, when she thought about passing over that cattleguard and going into the fields, she just…froze. She couldn't make herself open the gate.

After that happened a few times, she decided the impulse was her better angels telling her not to trespass on whoever's property was beyond that fence without permission, and she'd stopped trying to get to the stream.

Today, though, with the sun out and the breeze cool and flavored with greenery and autumn, with her frustration riding her hard, she considered the gate again. And the stream beyond. A walk through the shady trees near a bubbling brook sounded so idyllic. The very stuff of her Irish fantasies. Peaceful walks by brooks during the afternoon, lots of fiction written in the evening after those walks.

Maybe that's all she needed. To experience some of that Dream Ireland. To live the moments she'd imagined experiencing. Maybe that would help her creative brain open up and solve the bloody problems in her novel.

A crow flew overhead, its shadow making the sunlight flicker. She glanced up in time to see it swing past and bank over the fallow field before circling back and landing on the stone wall a hundred yards away. The crow cawed and ruffled its feathers.

Becks turned back to the gate, but the instant she set her hand to it, the moment her hand touched that metal, her body shivered and a sweep of what she could only call fear moved through her. Like crossing the cattleguard would bring out something terrible. The fear, the throat-clutching, stomach-churning, better-run-soon terror was so sudden, so swift, and so new she gasped and stepped back from the gate as if it had burned her.

What the actual hell?

She blinked and looked beyond the gate. And this time, instead of a sunny field of grass and a beautiful, tree-lined stream, fog rose up from the ground, covering the grass, obscuring the stream. Mist that looked like it had…something moving inside it. Shapes. Shapes that swirled. Shapes that moved.

Shapes that laughed.

Becks felt a scream crawling up her throat. She backed up so fast, her foot hit the edge of the pond, and she stepped into the water. The pond wasn't deep. The water only came up to her ankle. But between the shock of cold water filling her sneakers, and the almost child-like laughter coming from inside the strange mist, she did scream. Or more let out a strangled half-gasp, half-screech. She leapt out of the water as if something inside the pond might grab her and stumbled a few more steps toward the path back to her rental cottage.

When she looked at the pond, the surface settled like glass. Reflecting the bright blue sky overhead.

And when she looked back at the field…nothing but dark soil and green green grass, and a sunny, welcoming brook lined with trees beyond.

The crow cawed again and launched back into the air, circling off toward the village.

Becks stopped in her retreat to stare. What. The. Hell?

Was she losing her mind? Starting to hallucinate because she couldn't break out of her funk and just finish her damned novel?

This didn't feel like some sort of creative break through. The…whatever had just happened didn't suddenly solve her plot problems. She wasn't writing a spooky book.

She took a step back toward the stone fence, but even though the field remained sunny and pleasant and rocky looking, a hand of fear clenched her throat. Choking away her curiosity.

Becks spun around and headed back toward the cottage.

So much for a walk to clear her head. Now she was creeped out and confused.

And scared.

The noise came from the pond again that night. But this time it didn't sound like random feet-shuffling, muffled movement, like a sheep herd escaped. As she lay awake listening that night, it sounded more like… music and laughter. Like someone was throwing a party.

She wondered if all that racket was actually coming from the pond or from the field beyond. Maybe she should ask who owned the field at the pub. Ask if they were holding parties at night.

If all her bad sleep had been because of parties instead of sheep, though, wouldn't she have seen some evidence of that? Maybe the other nights had been sheep and this was a party?

There had to be a logical explanation, though. Flute music was weird, but she wouldn't put it past drunk partiers to be playing flutes. There had to be an explanation.

Even if some of the laughter she heard sounded suspiciously like the ghostly laughter she'd heard inside the mist that afternoon.

She stuffed pillows against her ears and tried to sleep.

The next day, she did go up to the pub for lunch after

another frustrating morning trying to write. She'd typed sentences, a lot of them, and none of them went anywhere. It was like she was that guy in that horror movie typing the same line over and over again. Except she wasn't typing the same line. She was typing different sentences. But they weren't taking her anywhere but in circles. They didn't make sense. They weren't solving the problem.

Frustration and annoyance had her pushing away from the computer again. Lunch at the pub. That's what she needed. Food and fuel. She was groggy from a bad night's sleep, her brain was tired, and coffee hadn't much helped. Not that the instant coffee she mixed with boiled kettle water really constituted coffee. If she wasn't already stretched financially from this trip, she'd consider buying a proper coffee machine and real coffee. But it seemed a luxury she didn't technically *need*.

Food wasn't a luxury, though. And lunch at the pub was a good deal.

So she told herself as she grabbed her purse and headed out, walking up the lane to the main road that ran through the village.

The sidewalk was narrow, and broken, but the colorful buildings bracketing the road were charming. Window boxes filled with flowers decorated several storefronts. The yarn shop and a used bookstore had chalk stands outside advertising sales. Most of the buildings were single story and either whitewashed or painted bright blues or maroon colors. A couple of places were two story, like the butcher's shop, but she couldn't tell if the upper floors were storage or apartments and hadn't thought to ask yet. The chemist had bright neon lights inside their front window, which felt like a shock of modern in the quaint village. Though, the cars lining the streets, narrowing the road through town to barely a single lane, sort of squashed the illusion of timelessness too.

The pub was at the bottom of the road, a building that stood on its own, and past it, another ten minute walk, she could just see the steeples of the local church. She heard the bells ring occasionally, when she paid attention enough to listen. She kept promising herself she'd walk down there one day and see if the inside was as pretty as the steeples in the distance looked.

Today was not that day, though. Today, she pushed into the dark interior of the pub. There were some wooden tables set up outside, with long benches, all painted a dark green. But the day was gray and drizzly so no one had taken advantage of the exterior tables.

What felt like half the village were all crammed inside the pub instead. She blinked at the number of people as she stood in the doorway waiting for her eyes to adjust to the dimness. There were windows along one wall of the pub, squares of bubbled glass that didn't seem to let much light inside. A long wooden bar lined one side of the large room, the rest was filled with round wooden tables and small booths against two of the remaining walls. The smell of the lunch buffet laid out in the middle of the pub, with sliced meets and potatoes and roasted vegetables competed with the hops of rich beer and decades-old smoke. Smoking wasn't allowed inside the pub anymore, and hadn't been for a while according to one irate smoker she'd spoken to, but the furniture and walls had seemed to absorb the smell.

The lunch buffet managed to override the smoke and beer smell enough to make her stomach growl. The pub did lay out a good lunch. The proprietor had hired the best cook in the county last year, and that meant her pub filled up regularly with locals and tourists alike looking for hearty, superb meals.

A handful of flatscreen TVs hung above the bar, one showing a rugby game, but the other four were all playing a sport that involved a stick that looked a little like a hockey stick and a round ball that either got bounced on the stick or batted to another player like a baseball.

Hurling. And a huge crowd. Must be Saturday. She hadn't even realized.

She wound through the throng, looking for a spare chair somewhere, scanning for familiar faces. She recognized a lot of the locals she'd met since arriving. But every seat in the house was occupied.

In the end, she had to settle for one of the tall stools at the bar. She didn't mind, though. She got her food, could still look up to see what was happening in the hurling match—though the shouts and cheers and curses from the crowd were pretty good indicators of what was going on—and she could chat with the lovely woman tending bar whenever Caoimhe got to pause pulling pints.

The noise from the game made real conversation impossible, though, so she waited until the end of the match, when the team the locals had been cheering for won by a point, and the conversation in the place settled into a collective drone of many quieter conversations.

"Hey," Becks greeted when the bartender settled against the bar next to her, idly wiping a glass dry like she was an extra in a movie and needed something to do with her hands. "Do you know anything about that field down from the cottage? I keep hearing stuff that sounds like someone's partying down there every night."

Caoimhe's eyebrows rose and she scanned the pub before leaning over the bar to get closer to Becks, setting the pint glass aside. "What kind of partying?"

Caoimhe was a youngish woman, maybe only a few years

older than Becks. But she'd lived in this village her whole life and was always good with a story. She kept her incredibly curly brown hair pulled back in a ponytail most of the time, and even in the dim lights behind the bar, the sprinkle of freckles over her pale skin was obvious.

It had only taken Becks two tries to be able to pronounce Caoimhe's name. So long as she didn't look at the spelling, she was fine. A name that sounded like Kweeva, shouldn't have an *m* in it. But Becks liked the traditional Irish names. They, for better or worse, fed into that Irish fantasy she'd traveled here with.

"I don't know," Becks answered Caoimhe's question. "There's music, although it sounds like flutes and stuff rather than dance music. And there's always a lot of laughter."

"Oh shite. You're hearing the laughter? That's not good."

"Why?"

"Are you seeing any evidence of a party in the morning?"

"I only heard the laughter and party last night and I didn't go down to the pond today. I've been hearing a lot of noise down there that sounds like sheep or something. But last night was the first night it sounded like a party."

"What happened yesterday?" Caoimhe leaned farther over the sticky wooden bar, getting her face close to Becks.

Becks found herself leaning closer to Caoimhe, lowering her voice to match Caoimhe's. "Nothing much. Went for a walk after getting in some writing." Trying to write anyway. "And thought I might walk by the stream, but—"

"Don't!" Caoimhe grabbed Becks' arm and squeezed tight. Her sharp word brought attention from some of the people sitting nearest them, but mostly they went ignored. Caoimhe lowered her voice again and leaned even closer. "Do *not* cross that cattleguard. Do you understand? Stay *this* side of that fence."

"Why? Does the owner get upset when you trespass on their field?"

"Something like that." The bartender winced. "Look, it's best you ignore all that going on in the field. Just ignore it. Better for everyone."

"Who is it, though? Someone dangerous?"

"Who... I couldn't say."

Though Becks got the feeling that was a lie.

"Dangerous...depends. If you ignore them, not dangerous at all. If you go down there and try to confront them... dangerous. Just leave it."

"It's been making sleep hard."

Caoimhe's brows lowered and she frowned deeply. "For how long?"

"About a week or so."

"Bollocks," Caoimhe muttered under her breath. Then, "Here. Set out a bowl with milk in it on your front step tonight. That might appease them and make them go away. A little bit of bread will go a long way to helping, too. Set those out for the rest of your stay. You should be fine."

A regular down the other end of the bar raised a hand to get Caoimhe's attention and the bartender straightened away from Becks. She waved to the regular, but before she moved away, she said, "Just set out the milk and bread. You should be safe enough."

And with that ominous attempt at comfort, Caoimhe went back to pulling pints.

Confused and more than a little freaked out, Becks left enough Euro on the bar to pay for her lunch and the single pint of Guinness she'd allowed herself, as well as a nice tip for Caoimhe, and headed out.

Rather than making her feel better and giving her a logical explanation for whatever was happening at the pond and in that field, the conversation had just left her feeling more disoriented and confused.

She did stop at the small grocery store, that was more like a convenience store at home, and picked up some milk and a fresh loaf of bread. She wouldn't have considered herself a superstitious type, but she wouldn't have considered herself *not* superstitious either. If Caoimhe thought leaving out bread and milk might help, she'd do it.

But she had no idea *why* something like that might help.

CHAPTER 3

*S*he had a series of calls that afternoon with her agent and her editor over the galley proof mishap, and then she decided she was still too upset and tired to write properly, so instead, she did a full internet search on what leaving out milk and bread on her doorstep might mean.

The search led her to fairies.

Fairies.

Unlike the Ireland of her imagination, the real Ireland was a lot more grounded than she'd expected. The people didn't go around telling fairy stories and warning about crossing weird streams or staying out at intersections at midnight. They were more likely to complain about politics and the latest motorway plans that would wreck the village, or fix the traffic depending on who you were. So to have been given a "fix" to her problem that involved something to do with fairies seemed more than a little strange.

Maybe they were taking the piss, as they said. Slagging her. Teasing her. Caoimhe wouldn't have done it to be mean. But the Irish did do a lot of ribbing and teasing each other. It was probably a sign the bartender liked her if she was taking the time to play a joke on her.

But Caoimhe had seemed so serious.

Caoimhe was young, though. The younger Irish generation were definitely *not* very superstitious. Maybe one of the old fellas that hung out at the pub might slag Becks by alluding to fairies, but any of the younger generation? Not likely.

So why was her research on the whole milk and bread thing leading to fairies?

Maybe it was just a town superstition?

Caoimhe had said that whoever was doing all the partying in the field was dangerous, though. Becks had imagined a biker gang or something. Not that she'd seen a biker gang in Ireland yet, but she supposed it was possible.

More plausible than fairies.

Still, as the evening wore on, and she read more and more Irish myths about fairies—most of which were either filled with terrorizing stories, or implied the fairies were mischievous but could be appeased—the thought of them took hold. Got into her head in a way that felt...

Well, felt like the Ireland she'd expected to find. That dream place. A place of myths, legends, and...fairies.

Just before bed, she pulled out a ceramic plate and bowl, filled the bowl with milk, put a few slices of bread—they called it pan here—onto a plate. Wondered if a couple of slices was enough. Decided if it wasn't, she'd know about it by morning.

The front of the cottage was a small paved courtyard that was technically a driveway surrounded by a brick fence but with no gate to close off the driveaway/courtyard. There were two steps up front of the door, and a couple of planters on either side of the steps that, she imagined, bloomed with flowers in the spring, but this late in the autumn were mostly just weeds. She had a rental car she parked in the driveway but found she only drove it when absolutely necessary because driving a stick shift—which she wasn't used to—on the wrong side of the road—which she *really* wasn't used to —was terrifying.

Bowl and plate in hand, she set the whole collection just outside her front door. But as she stood there, thinking about *fairies* coming that close to her front door, she started to freak out. So she pushed the bowl and plate to the bottom of the two steps that led up to the cottage, so that they were sitting on the driveway. Still pretty close to her front door.

She considered setting the whole thing by the edge of the driveway, near the brick fence. That would keep the… whoever the milk and bread was for from having to come near the cottage.

Tempting. Very tempting. She didn't have any nearby neighbors to notice and slag her for falling for a fairytale. And it would mean the…whoever would never have to come onto her property at all.

But most of the tales had been pretty specific about the milk and bread being out on a stoop or doorstep, not at the base of the driveway.

She glanced out to the left, to the path that led down to the pond and beyond that, the gate and cattleguard that crossed into a fallow field where she wasn't supposed to trespass.

Since it was dark, and there were no streetlights in the area, she couldn't see any of that. She could barely see the road in front of the house. There were a few scattered stars overhead, but clouds scuttered over the sky, blocking those. There was no moon up yet. And the nearest houses were just far enough away to look more like light dots. They did nothing to illuminate the surroundings.

A crow cawed from somewhere nearby, but she couldn't see it in the blackness.

Until just that moment, she'd found the lack of light pollution and quiet darkness welcoming. A nice reprieve from her usual life. But as she stared down toward where the pond and fallow field were, the darkness took on a heavier, scarier weight.

Okay. Milk and bread on the stoop for tonight.

She shut the door, locked it, and went to bed trying to convince herself the milk and bread were just going to attract stray animals or dogs. She'd end up with a collection of squirrels waiting for their tribute by morning. The thought amused her, helped ease some of the fear that had been nipping at her consciousness since coming back from the pub. She felt silly about the milk and bread as she went to bed.

Until she heard the sounds of music and laughter.

CHAPTER 4

*B*ecks woke with a sense of disorientation. It took her several minutes of staring up at the ceiling of her small bedroom before her brain settled from strange dreams she couldn't remember. She'd slept. Soundly. Hard. For the first time in more than a week. She remembered hearing the music again, the laughter and noise. But then…

She didn't remember falling asleep, but obviously she had and deeply.

The memory of the bowl of milk and plate of bread left on the stoop rose, and she buried her face in her pillow, glad she didn't have any neighbors to notice her doing that. How embarrassing. A real "American" moment. She'd take a ribbing from Caoimhe next time she went into the pub for sure.

She wasn't entirely surprised to find the bowl and plate empty when she went out to collect them, though. This time, the thought of squirrels or other animals coming up to her stoop to eat the food left her a bit icked out. She was going to bring rodents to her door, maybe get the cabin infested with mice.

The idea made her shiver. She wasn't a fan of mice inside her house. Didn't mind them out in the fields where they belonged, but she didn't want them in the house.

She washed the plate and bowl by hand after breakfast, put everything away, and pushed all thoughts of fairies and mice to the back of her head so she could attempt to write.

Only, attempting turned into actually writing that day. Real words that felt right and flowed and suddenly all the issues she'd had with her plot seemed to open up in front of her, laying the path forward, giving way to the story she'd been desperately trying to find and not being able to figure out.

Her writing sessions were so productive, she forgot to eat lunch. She blinked hard when the light in the room seemed suddenly dim. She looked at a clock and realized it was so late in the afternoon, it was almost time for dinner. She hadn't even checked her email yet.

The excellent writing day left her nearly giddy.

Washing up after dinner, she considered the bowl and plate she'd left out the night before. Without thinking too hard about it, she filled the bowl with milk, added a few more slices of pan to the plate, and left the whole lot at the base of her stoop. Locked the front door. And went to bed trying not to think about mice.

THE WRITING FLOW CONTINUED INTO THE NEXT DAY, AND THE next. Becks only realized on the fourth day that she was out of bread and milk. But by the time she realized, it was after eight at night and everything was closed. Short of driving a long distance to find a store that might be open—an unlikely scenario—she decided one night without the milk and bread wouldn't hurt too much.

She went to bed with her head full of her novel and the direction it was headed. Full of the words and scenes and images that she knew she'd be working on the next day.

And she drifted off to the sound of distant laughter.

The next morning, she discovered a strange sort of growth on the front stoop. A black mold that hadn't been there the day before. Given how damp Ireland was, she wasn't entirely surprised by the mold. But she also didn't want to let it go. So she gave up one of her two writing sessions that morning to take a trip to the shop.

She had to ask around to find something that worked for black mold, but was assured that sort of thing wasn't uncommon. By the time she got home, she realized she'd forgotten all about needing bread and milk. But the words were still flowing and she'd gotten a good night sleep. She could probably give up the superstition now. Whatever had been in that field, or even if it was just some of the younger people in the village taking the piss, she was sure all that was done. She didn't want to take more time away from the writing. The book was due soon. And she'd spent a lot of money on this dream retreat. She was here to write, not pretend fairies existed.

She treated her front stoop for the mold as a crow watched her closely from the brick fence. Then she went back to writing.

And slept well again that night, although she swore she heard some scratching at the front door right before she drifted off. Probably mice. Good thing she hadn't put out the bread and milk.

THE NEXT MORNING, SHE FELT A BIT MORE SLUGGISH, BUT THE words were still there. She didn't even look out the front door until after lunch when she knew she needed to get some natural light into her eyes, even if it was sunlight filtered through a heavy cloud cover.

The door stuck when she tried to open it and it took a few good tugs before she wrenched it free.

Only to discover more of the black mold. This time growing up over the door and along the stoop. There were cracks in the steps that hadn't been there the day before, and the mold lines along the blue door had overlapped enough of the doorjamb to nearly seal it closed.

That was terrifying.

She hurried back into the village, back to the hardware store where she'd picked up the mold killer spray the day before. As she was talking to the older man behind the counter, Caoimhe came into the shop and overheard her mention mold.

"Have you been leaving out the milk and bread?" she asked, very seriously.

The man behind the counter gave Caoimhe a frown. "What's this, then?"

"She's been hearing…stuff down the old fallow field, past the cattleguard," Caoimhe told him.

The man's eyebrows rose into his shaggy white hair. "Why didn't ye tell me about that? This mold killer won't help with that sort of thing. You need the milk and bread fer that."

Becks frowned at the two. "For mold? Seems like that would just give the mold more to…eat."

To Becks' surprise, Caoimhe shivered. "You need to listen to what we're telling you. You have to leave out the milk and bread. No missing now. It's too late to get out of it. The minute they started dancing down there, the minute ye heard them, you needed to start laying out their offering. You don't…" Caoimhe pulled herself up with a deep breath, let it out slowly. "Well, I'm just saying, you need to leave out the offering. You do that, ye'll have no worries at all at all."

The warning reminded Becks of the sound of scratching at her door last night. "But what if all that is attracting mice? I swear I heard scratching at the door."

Another look exchanged between the owner of the hardware store and Caoimhe. "It's not too late. Don't you worry about mice. That's the least of it. Just leave out the offering."

"And what do I do about the mold?" This Becks directed at the man behind the counter. He pushed up his thin-rimmed glasses and shrugged. "Ye can spray it again with the stuff I gave you yesterday. But the offering will do better than anything I can sell you."

Certain they were still making fun of her, Becks left with a sigh. But she did go right to the shop to pick up more bread and milk.

And that night, despite the mold that seemed to have spread even more during the day, despite the spray she covered it in, she left the bowl of milk and a few slices of bread on a plate at the bottom of the steps up to the door.

There was no laughter, or scratching, or music that night. No sound at all.

Which was almost as unnerving as the sounds had been.

CHAPTER 5

*B*ecks woke to bright sunshine spilling in through her small bedroom window, and a vague memory of strange dreams that didn't quite stick in her memory. She recalled something about a bonfire. And dancing. But none of it pulled up as clear when she tried to recapture the images from the dream.

She was tired, though. Groggier than she expected after a full night's sleep. It took several cups of coffee and a semi-cold shower to get her moving that morning.

The words came that day, still flowing out of her, but she found herself trying to fall asleep in her laptop. When she woke suddenly, her chin resting on her chest, her fingers resting against the keyboard, with a series of ooooooooooooo's in the document on screen following the last word she remembered writing, she decided she'd better take a nap.

She forgot to check the front door and the mold until after the nap.

When she tugged at the door, it opened smoothly, no

resistance at all. Her heart started to pound a little harder as she stepped outside to see no sign of the black mold. Or the cracks in the steps that had been there the day before. The walls around the door were clean and white. The blue paint on the door looked unblemished. It was as if the mold had never been there.

And the milk and bread were gone, the plate and bowl empty.

A tremor of something close to fear moved up Becks' spine. She tried to shake it off. She'd sprayed the hell out of the mold the day before. Of course it was gone now. That mold killer spray was full of bleach and chemicals that were deadly to mold. It was just a coincidence that the very night she put the bread and milk out again happened to be the night the spray finally finished the job. She probably just hadn't used enough the other day.

A sharp caw from a crow overhead had her jumping and ducking back inside fast, despite feeling ridiculous for her fear.

To calm her nerves, she kept repeating the logic that the mold killer had finally worked to herself throughout the afternoon, as the writing once again flowed. At this rate, she'd make her deadline with a few weeks to spare. She could enjoy her last couple of weeks in Ireland without the pressure of the book deadline looming over her, maybe even do some sightseeing.

The exhaustion still dragged at her all afternoon, though, so she ended her work day early, finishing up with a few business emails. Ate an easy dinner of cheese and cream crackers, then went to bed. She was just starting to drift off when she remembered the milk and bread.

With a groan, and an admonishment to her logical brain to shut the hell up, she went back to the kitchen, got the milk and bread, and set them out at the bottom stoop. Then locked the door behind her and stumbled back to bed.

THE MOLD DIDN'T RETURN. BECKS' WRITING CONTINUED TO flow. Each night, she remembered the milk and bread, never again allowing distraction or tiredness to keep her from making the offering.

But the exhaustion got worse. And her dreams grew progressively more vivid and strange.

There was always a bonfire. Music. Dancing. She had flashes of faces in the firelight. Laughter that swirled around her. Nothing she could recall in detail the next day. Just impressions and images that, when looked at in bright morning sunlight, scared her. She was never scared in the dreams. Only when she woke up and thought back on them did the creep of fear rush through her blood.

By the time she'd finished her coffee, checked the front door for mold and to retrieve the empty bowl and plate, showered and readied for her day, even those vague memories of the dreams faded. She worked so hard, her fingers and back ached from not remembering to stand often enough. But that didn't seem to stop her from writing. Words flowing so fast she was surprised her typing kept up with them.

When the first really cold day of autumn hit, forcing her to turn on the heat, she realized she was almost done with the novel. Written faster and easier than any novel before. Once the dam had broken on her thorny plot problems, the rest had spilled out of her hands like water.

To celebrate being at her very last scene, and for the first time in weeks, Becks decided to take a walk down to the pond during her lunch break. She hadn't been since that day dread had kept her from crossing the cattleguard. It was a lot colder on this walk, with a sharp breeze blowing through the fields, bringing with it the flavor of frost. The ground was harder, the damp dirt path frozen and slippery in places, forcing her to walk slowly and carefully. The evergreens held green against the gray skies, but the grass was covered in a frosty coating that made it look white. The pond itself was frozen over, the glossy surface reflecting the sky, a smoked mirror, the edges blurred like Venetian glass.

Becks pulled her coat tighter around her. She was used to snowy cold winters, but this was her first experience of real cold here in Ireland, and it changed the landscape and her view of the place in unexpected ways. Honestly, she'd never thought about Ireland as frosty cold. Her imagination and fantasy of the place had always been nothing but green fields and stone walls and thatched roof cottages.

She found she liked the reality better than her fantasy, now that the words were flowing.

But the sight of the fallow field covered in ice left her... edgy. Uncomfortable. And she wasn't sure why. She strolled close to the gate, remaining on this side of the cattleguard, but she did reach out and wrap a hand around one of the gate's horizontal bars, the rough metal icy against her bare skin.

Weak sunlight covered the frosted field in a dimness that didn't feel like it matched the rest of the countryside. From the direction of the stream, Becks could swear she saw shadows moving through the trees. And laughter floated across the field. She leaned against the gate as a wave of exhaustion swept through her, her head bobbing as cold and tiredness sank into her bones. She lurched back to wakefulness when she felt her cheek touch the icy railing and the gate start to swing open.

Stumbling with the sudden loss of resistance, she found

herself clinging to the gate, standing in the middle of the cattleguard, the metal lines through the dirt beneath her barely close enough for her foot to extend from one tie to the next. If she turned her foot the wrong way, it could easily slip between the grate. But that wasn't what made her freeze, her body trembling.

She froze when she realized she was halfway to crossing that don't-cross barrier and entering the fallow field.

Mist rose up from the ice, though she wasn't sure how that was possible given how cold the ground was. Still that mist rose, covering the field so she could no longer see the icy grass and dirt, just a blanket of gray-white fog. The stream on the other side of the field seemed to get farther away, as if the space between her and it stretched in some sort of weird movie special effect.

Laughter. Louder now. And she could swear she heard her name. Someone was calling her? Who the hell would be out here now? Maybe it was Caoimhe? No, that sounded wrong. Caoimhe had told her not to cross the cattleguard.

The air tasted different now too, though Becks could explain what it was about it. Like sugar and electricity. Like flowers and dirt and a hint of…sulfur?

The gate slipped open farther and she took another stumbling step over the cattleguard, closer to the field. The laugher got louder. When she looked down, the fog edged closer to her feet, but it didn't cross the metal bars of the guard. Which was, she realized in some lizard part of her brain, not the way fog worked.

She frowned at the stream. More shadows among the trees, obscured by the fog, but she'd swear they were beaconing her, waving for her to join them, calling her name.

Her foot slipped farther along the cattleguard, closer to the edge of the field.

The air around her felt charged and yet soft. Her skin prickled. An urge to laugh filled her. She chuckled. And a giddy delight rolled through her.

She stepped to the very edge of the cattleguard. The metal beneath her tennis shoes felt weirdly warm. Almost like it was burning through her shoes. That seemed wrong given all the frost everywhere. Shouldn't the metal be cold.

Maybe it was. Maybe it was the cold that was burning, the way the cold metal of the gate stung her hand.

She focused on that sting. She was still holding the gate. The section she held should have been warmed enough not to feel so cold now. But her hand felt almost glued to the gate, like to move it would rip off her skin.

That thought made her shiver.

More laughter. And now she was sure she heard her name, a soft calling on the sharp breeze.

Her foot slipped forward again, though it didn't feel like a conscious move. Her toes hung at the edge of the cattleguard, almost touching the fog beyond.

Inside the fog on the fields, little sparks of light danced, swirled, caught in the breeze. Laughter. Faces?

She looked down to the mist reaching out to her, like slim fingers on a pale white hand.

With her free hand, Becks reached out toward the mist, toward that hand reaching for her.

And then something hard landed on her shoulder.

Becks blinked hard a few times as she stumbled backward, back over the cattleguard, away from the reaching fog.

The laughter stopped abruptly. The whispered sound of her name no more than an ordinary breeze. Above a crow cawed, dipping and passing just over Becks' head, close enough she ducked.

Then turned to see Caoimhe standing there, glaring up at the crow. "What'd'ya think you were doing there?" she asked, but with her glare on the crow it was hard to tell if she was talking to Becks or the bird.

Becks answered. "Just stretching my legs."

Caoimhe's gaze dropped to hers. "What did I tell ye about crossing the cattleguard? The…owners of that land would not be pleased." She scowled over the field.

Becks glanced over her shoulder. The fog was gone now, as if it had never been there. The field was still frost-covered, looking icy and slippery, but there were no more dancing lights, or mist. And no laughter.

"Might be too pleased, more like," Caoimhe muttered.

"What?" Becks faced the bartender again, clearing her throat when her voice came out rough, like she'd been yelling for hours. "What was that?"

Caoimhe waved a hand in the air. "Just stay out of that field." She stared hard into Becks' face for a moment. "You haven't been sleeping again?"

"No, I have. Just…weird dreams."

"Dreams. Sure. Grand, so." Caoimhe glared at the field again. "Come on. Think you could do with a drink."

Becks followed Caoimhe, shaken for reasons she couldn't quite pinpoint. She happily drank all three pints Caoimhe put in front of her that afternoon. And slept without dreaming that night after putting out her bread and milk.

CHAPTER 6

The next morning, Becks finished her novel, though getting that last scene out felt like pulling teeth again, the words no longer flowing. But she managed to get it done, closing the document with a deep, relieved sigh. After backing everything up and sending the draft to her agent, she finally went to collect the plate and bowl from last night.

The milk still filled the bowl, covered with a slight crust of frost. The bread, also covered in shiny crystals, remained untouched.

Becks frowned and looked out to the road past the brick fence encircling the paved front yard. Then she looked at her door and the wall around the door. No black mold. Everything looked as it should. Everything was exactly as it was the night before.

She stepped far enough outside to look down the road toward the pond, toward the cattleguard and the field beyond. She couldn't see the field well, or the pond. Just the general area. But there was no mist or anything. No laughter.

As she moved back toward the cottage a crow flew overhead, dipping its wings toward her and cawing before landing on a nearby telephone line. She stared up at the crow. It cawed at her again and then took to the air, flying off into the distance.

Becks went back into the cottage and spent the rest of the day packing her bags and making arrangements for a hotel in Dublin, changing her flights home so she left in a week, letting her landlord know she needed to leave early. She went to the pub for dinner so she could say goodbye to Caoimhe and let her know she was leaving early. Caoimhe didn't even ask why or seem surprised by the change of plan. They chatted while Becks ate and had one final pint, then said their goodbyes at the end of the evening.

The next day, Becks drove away from the cottage, carefully trying not to grind the gears on her rental's standard transmission, carefully reminding herself to stay on the correct side of the road.

Never looking back toward the pond or the field beyond the cattleguard.

Even when she heard the sound of laughter.

THE TROLL AND THE
DRESSMAKER

CHAPTER 1

*E*veryone knew about the troll under the bridge. There weren't a lot of trolls in our area, so when one moved in under the only bridge leading into our village, of course we all noticed. Hard to miss something like that. Trolls have a really distinctive smell. Nothing horrible, or anything. You get used to it. But it's definitely nothing you can mistake for anything else. Bit like burnt wood and badger combined. Weird. Little ripe. But manageable.

The troll was pretty shy. None of this "feed me your goats" business. Just hung out quietly, listening to the horse carts moving past overhead. Occasionally, when children danced across the bridge, he'd throw a few pretty stones up onto the wooden planks for them to find. Little treasures to take home and tell stories about.

Apparently, the troll liked stories. One of the villagers, walking across with a friend, told a big whopper of a story about his cousin up in the palace, who worked in one of the princesses' wings, catching a curtain on fire while he was trying to clean out a wardrobe. The story was ridiculous and half made up—I'm pretty sure Jordan's cousin works in the kitchens, not anywhere near the royal family—but Jordan's a good storyteller and he had Amas laughing all the way across the bridge.

According to Jordan, he spotted the troll's eye peeking out through one of the knots in a plank, blinking up at him as they passed the halfway point in the bridge. And by the time they reached the opposite side of the bridge, there was a small pile of pretty stones waiting for him.

Not just any stones either. These were lovely blue and yellow stones, the kind that washed down occasionally during rainstorms from the high mountains to the east. Nothing like them in our stream unless there's been a storm, so they're considered pretty valuable, at least in our community. Jordan figured he was nearly as rich as the royals after that. He was soon disabused of that notion when Farmer Ren wouldn't give him change for a blue stone after he traded for some milk and cheese with it.

Not that we take pleasure in bringing our own back down to the earth after they get notions, but yeah, some of us enjoy bringing our own back to earth after they get notions. And Jordan is, unfortunately, a little predisposed to getting notions. I guess that comes with being a storyteller—or what Farmer Ren often calls a "liar."

Me, I'm just a dressmaker. I live near the center of town, and I like telling stories too, but I don't tell the elaborate ones Jordan does. I like the silly stories, like the ones the kids tell about dragons and unicorns and stuff. All those strange animals that live in the neighboring kingdom that no one from our village has actually seen. I've been telling those kinds of stories for years to my clients as they sit for the, sometimes laborious, process of getting pinned. Arianna once told me that's the whole reason she starting coming to me for dresses, because I tell stories and make the standing still and not fidgeting during a pinning easier. Which is kind of her to say. But in all honesty, I'm the only dressmaker in the village, so I think she was just being nice.

Anyway, the troll lived under our bridge for maybe a month before I found myself having to cross that particular bridge. So I hadn't encountered him at all. Just the smell when I walked by, that strangely troll smell. After hearing about all the rocks being left for the storytellers, I figured the troll would remain friendly and therefore nothing we needed to alert the castle about if we kept telling him stories. So even though I was alone, I told this story about a unicorn getting its horn stuck in a melon and bouncing all over the place trying to get it off. It was a ridiculous story, a silly one that made my clients giggle if I wasn't careful—giggle too much they get stuck with a pin! I let rip for the troll, though, including all the silly antics I could come up with. Lots of unicorn bumping off walls, plowing into trees, tripping over badgers trying to be helpful. That kind of thing.

I was over the bridge before I realized I hadn't gotten any response from the troll. Hadn't even seen him. Certainly no rocks left out for me.

Well. I guess I wasn't the storyteller—liar—Jordan was or the children. Ah well. At least no goats were demanded. I didn't have any convenient goats to feed a troll.

I left the village to go into the next village within walking distance to deliver a specially made outfit for a baby just born to one of my friends who used to live in our village. She'd moved when she married and was now happily part of her new community. But when she came back to visit her family, we always managed to get together for tea and have a good gossip. I hadn't had a chance to tell her about the troll yet, so I was looking forward to that.

Her daughter had been born about two months ago, and

I'd gone immediately to deliver some food and a new blanket for mother and newborn. But I hadn't been back since. The finished little dress for her daughter was my excuse to close my own shop and take the day to visit and make sure she was doing well.

Molly was sitting by the fire when I reached her house, a small cottage at the edge of the village closest to the road leading up to the castle. It was early spring and still a little chilly outside, but the cottage had all the windows wide open, letting in the lovely cool breeze.

Molly rose from her chair, giving the cradle by her chair a little push so it continued rocking before greeting me.

"Angel is asleep," she murmured, giving me a hug. "We'll have to be quiet. I'm so glad you came for a visit."

She looked tired, circles under her dark eyes like little purple patches against her dark brown skin. She had a scarf wrapped around her curly hair, keeping it all up and off her neck. And she had some spit up on her serviceable blue wool shirt and trousers. But otherwise, she looked good.

We sat outside the cottage on a long wooden bench, with the door left open so she could hear the baby, and had a good, quiet chat over dark, rich tea and flaky shortbread biscuits set out on a pewter plate between us. The dress I'd made for her daughter was still too big, which was good—I'd been afraid it would be just right and they'd only get a week's wear from it before Angel outgrew it. Her husband was at his place of business—he owned the foods and goods store; Molly had married well—so we were free to gossip about everything. And we did.

She was pretty astonished to hear about the troll. But she was even more astonished to hear I hadn't gotten a stone for my story.

"I love that clumsy unicorn story!" She raised her voice a

little too much and after a frantic look back into the cottage, where Angel remained asleep thankfully, she said more quietly, "I can't image that story was any less entertaining than anything Jordan Beels would have to say."

She sniffed a little at mention of Jordan. They'd once fancied each other, when we were kids, but Jordan had decided he preferred Emma Haveeve, and Molly had decided Jordan was horse dung. And she'd held a grudge ever since, even though they were both happily married now, and she'd married a wealthy merchant who was also an extremely kind man.

"Maybe I just didn't tell my story well enough." I shrugged. "So long as the troll is happy and not demanding livestock, I'm happy."

"Still. Those yellow and blue rocks from up the east mountains are beautiful. Remember in school, that story the witch told us about how the rocks can be put at doors and windows for protection?"

I hadn't thought of that tale in years.

"Here," Molly continued, "they say the rocks can have magic in them. Or maybe it's that magic can be put in them. I don't remember. Thinking is fuzzy these days." She smiled and nodded back inside. "This is the longest she's slept since being born. I'm pretty tired."

I sat up a little. "Do you need some help? Should I see if Bethany can come for a few weeks?" Bethany was Molly's younger sister and just finished up with her schooling a week ago. I was pretty sure their parents would approve Bethany having something useful to do with her time because at the moment she was threatening to move closer to the castle and no one wanted that.

"I'm fine," Molly assured. "This part doesn't last long. So I've been reassured by Maneesh's sisters. They come over regularly to help and let me sleep. But Angel is mine so I'm protective of her."

"Let me know if you need more help. I can close up the shop for a week, too."

Molly waved my offer away and moved into village gossip, effectively ending the conversation. Angel woke up not long after we'd finished our second cup of tea. I visited with the baby for a little bit and then left them to their evening routine.

The walk home was uneventful. And the trip over the bridge, during which I told another silly story, resulted in no rocks.

If I wasn't careful, I'd start to take that personally.

CHAPTER 2

Three weeks later, I had call to cross the bridge again. This time, I was heading up to the castle with cart in tow to collect some specific bolts of silk I needed—material that didn't regularly travel with the merchants. I had to go to it. But it was impossible to beat for certain things, like certain undergarments and the linings of coats and things. So once every few months, weather permitting, I made the trip.

I didn't particularly like going up round the castle. The royals and their ilk were all well and good, but at a distance. Where I didn't have to encounter their guards and their sycophants, and where I didn't have to watch that display of wealth that could have been put to better use.

Yes, I have *ideas* about this kind of thing.

Anyway, I considered not telling the troll a story as I crossed the bridge because I was grumpy already about my trip and because the troll didn't seem to like my stories anyway. He didn't demand goats for crossing. Didn't pester anyone who crossed without telling stories. Really, he was quite an easy troll to live with. No one minded having him under our bridge.

But as I hit the thick wooden slates passing over the river, I gave in. I couldn't help it. I knew he was listening. I spotted that huge green eye peeking out from a knot hole in the wood near the far edge of the bridge. He didn't look over the sides, or really show himself beyond that clue that he was watching. Still, the minute I knew he was listening, I gave in and told a story as I walked my single horse cart across.

I had to do a little calming of my horse, because this was her first time over the bridge since the troll had moved in. Horses don't typically like trolls, as you might imagine. But the ones who had to cross the bridge regularly had gotten used to our troll and didn't fuss anymore. Butter was still well inside the "fussing" stage of her acquaintance with troll smells.

So I spoke calmly, telling a soothing story about starlight falling from the sky and landing on a sleeping girl who then turned into a magical being. It was a story my little sister, Emma, had loved when we were kids, and I could tell it in a tone of voice that was quiet and calm and soothing.

By the time I got to the far end of the bridge, murmuring about magical winged beings who flew on moonbeams, Butter was calm and clomped along the wood without shying and jumping at every bird chirp.

There were no rocks, though.

Guess the troll didn't like soothing stories that calmed children and horses.

Not really sure what stories the troll would like, to be honest, but it was obviously not anything I knew or could tell. Just as well, I supposed. The blue and yellow rocks were valuable up near the castle. If I'd had any on me, a merchant might assume I had more wealth than I did and overcharge me for the silk. There were thieves on the roads too, and in the city surrounding the castle. Better to have only what I needed while I was there.

Which was a story I kept telling myself the whole trip so I wouldn't allow the troll's judgment of my stories to bother me.

Obviously, I wasn't bothered. Why should I be? He was just a troll under the bridge after all.

On the way back from my successful purchase of a dozen bolts of silk and no run-ins with thieves or crooked merchants or—even better!—no royals, I stopped in my friend Molly's village to visit with her for an hour while I rested Butter for the last leg of the journey home.

Angel was just getting over a cold, so she was fussy and Molly looked even more haggard than she had the last time I was there.

"She's fine now," Molly assured me as she cradled Angel on her lap while we sat outside enjoying the early autumn sunshine.

The late day light slanted directly against the side of Molly's cottage, where the long bench was, bouncing off the whitewashed walls of her home and warming us all in that lovely way only autumn sun can do. The breeze cooled as the sun dipped lower in the sky, carrying with it the woodsy smells of the neighbors' cooking fires.

"I just haven't slept much in the last week," Molly continued. "Hard to sleep when she couldn't because her nose was stuffy. The first day, when she had fever, that was the worst for me. I think she hated the last few days the most." She smiled down at the three-month-old as she coughed and then grabbed at the air with chubby little hands when a clarybug zoomed past, making its chittering chirp call.

"She looks happy enough now," I said, letting Angel grab my finger and squeeze it tight. "And she's still strong."

Molly grinned. "Once she can sleep again, I'll sleep again."

"While I'm here, let me make you all dinner," I said. And refused to let Molly refuse the offer.

We shared a lovely meal of venison stew and bread that Molly's sisters-in-law had brought over that morning. Her husband took over minding a still wide-awake Angel as Molly went to take a short nap. And I headed out after leaving them with a cleaned and tidied kitchen, kissing Angel on the head as I left.

It was dark by the time Butter and I and the cart full of silk bolts reached the bridge. Butter still wasn't happy about the troll smell, though, and balked harder at crossing the bridge in the dark than she had during the day. All smell, no vision at this time of night, the old mare. And the scent of troll was strong.

Stronger to me as well. I frowned a little as we stood just before the bridge, Butter resistant to setting hoof onto the wooden slats. And realized this was the first time I'd had cause to cross the bridge in the dark.

The moon was a large squished sphere, not quite full, but enough of it to cast some light on the road. The village was alight beyond the bridge since it was still early in the evening. Noise from the pub and the coaching inn, both on this side of the village, filtered over the river. Plenty of people still awake and moving around. Nothing particularly sinister in the area.

Just a stronger scent of troll.

I hunted the surroundings but there didn't seem to be any large beings walking along the shore of the river or lumbering up onto the road. Really, I couldn't tell you what our bridge troll looked like. I'd seen pictures in books of course, drawings done by people who claimed to have seen more than one troll. But since we didn't have many in this region, I'd never seen one out in the open before. Smelled them occasionally, but never seen one.

Still, I tried looking around, just to see if the smell was stronger because the troll was out from under the bridge. But nothing in the area looked changed or altered. No large piles of rocks that shouldn't be there. No movement beyond the rumbling of the river over smooth riverbed rocks. This late in the year, the river was low, and in the daytime, you could sometimes see the schools of silver fish swimming around. Come spring, the river would fill so much with snow runoff, it would rise high enough to occasionally be a threat to the bridge. But this time of year, the river was low and far away from the bottom of the bridge. Leaving lots of room beneath.

More than one troll, maybe? That would be unusual. Trolls were solitary. I'm not sure if anyone even knew how they reproduced. But as far as the books and the people who were supposed to know about this stuff were concerned, trolls only ever lived alone.

Butter restlessly tugged at the halter as I stood beside her. I couldn't afford to let her bolt with the cart strapped to her, and not just because I'd lose all that silk material I just bought. I didn't want Butter hurt. And to be honest, I didn't want to trigger the troll's hunting instincts. Or whatever trolls have that made them demand goats and payment for crossing bridges.

I held the halter close to Butter's cheek, soothing her with quiet words and gentle strokes along her long nose with my free hand. Nothing popped out of the darkness. Nothing appeared suddenly on the bridge. Nothing walked along the river shoreline.

Well and maybe it was just because it was nighttime.

Maybe trolls smelled stronger at night. I couldn't imagine why but then I was a dressmaker not a troll expert. I was sure there was someone somewhere who'd written a book about it and they'd probably know.

When Butter was calm enough to move forward and I'd assured myself there was nothing creeping around out from under the bridge, we started down the wooden slats. The cart creaked over the even wood—our bridge was strong and well-constructed thanks to Yian and Mosh, our two resident builders—and Butter's feet clomp clomped quietly even as she whinnied softly. The whites of her eyes shown in the dim moonlight. She snorted once or twice and pulled at the halter once so hard I had to pause to keep from getting pulled off the ground, settling her a bit more before moving on.

Halfway across the bridge, I decided I needed to pay my story toll, so I quietly gave the troll a simple story about a butterfly befriending a spider who spun the butterfly new, indestructible wings after her own got damaged in a storm. It was the sort of story I would tell to Angel or another baby while trying to get them to sleep. Nothing complicated, no complex morals or even ridiculous ribaldry. Nothing so silly it might make anyone laugh. Just a simple little story about helping someone in trouble, told in my most soothing and quiet murmur.

We made it to the other side of the bridge without incident. Though when we had only a few yards left to go, I did hear a large thump. A rock falling into the river bed maybe? I couldn't tell. And there wasn't enough light to see what had happened. Nothing came up onto the bridge, though. So I told myself it was a larger rock hitting another rock in the stream and hurried the rest of the way across the bridge.

There were no stones left for me for my story, but I

wasn't surprised by that anymore. I was just glad to be across safely, and on my way home.

I did glance back once, when Butter and I were almost inside the first houses of the village, their whitewashed walls and thick wooden roofs a comforting embrace after the journey. A shadow hovered just to one side of the bridge. Nothing I could see clearly. Might have even been imagining it. Just a thick patch of darkness that had no reason to be in that exact spot beside the bridge.

I blinked and the shadow was gone.

Trick of the moonlight, I assured myself and Butter as I turned back toward home.

CHAPTER 3

They found the remains of the beast the next morning farther down river. A mountain atti-wolf —though they weren't really wolves. Nothing like an ordinary wolf. The atti-wolves were huge, the size of a horse, and had razor sharp claws and teeth. Red eyes. Sometimes even walked on two legs. Their fur was said to ripple and they could fling it off like little needs. If the needles hit you, so the legend went, you'd be paralyzed, though not dead when the atti-wolf started eating you.

They never came down this far into the valley, and certainly not this close to our villages. They hadn't been seen in the area for as long as our eldest village member, Ms. Uma, had been alive and she was older than the rocks. Trolls had been in the area more recently than atti-wolves—our current troll excepted—and trolls were, as I've said, really really rare.

The sight of the giant animal, its neck broken, caught in some branches beside the stream became the talk of the village. How had it gotten here? Why was it here? How had it died?

The stories got more and more elaborate over the next two days. But no one had any answers. They brought the atti-wolf's body, very carefully to avoid the needle spines mixed into its fur, into the village so the doctor and the vet could examine it. Dr. Evers, the people doctor, was surprised how much an atti-wolf's body structure resembled a human's more than a wolf's. She deferred to Dr. Green, the vet, but Dr. Green couldn't provide much more helpful information. They agreed the neck of the beast was broken. They had no idea how it had happened.

One thing I noticed, as the atti-wolf's body sat in the middle of the village square while we all gathered around to watch the examination... The smell of the beast. It was musty, and there was the hint of rot that came with death, and some of the fishy-algae smell that came when the river was low like it is now. But there was also that distinct, impossible to mistake for anything else, smell of troll.

"Do atti-wolves smell like trolls usually?" I asked Dr. Green.

She frowned at me a little, pushing her glasses up her nose, and turned back to the wolf. She was an excellent vet. She'd even managed to save Erin Horis's best cow when the cow was birthing a breech, just last week. She'd even saved the calf. But atti-wolves weren't the typical animal most village vets dealt with.

"Far as I remember from my days at university," Dr. Green said, "atti-wolves and trolls aren't related even though they live in the same mountain range. They shouldn't have any reason to smell alike."

"Anyone else smell troll stronger around the wolf?" I asked the village at large. "Or is that just me?"

A lot of murmuring went up around the gathered villagers. A lot of nodding and mumbled, "She's right, you know." And "Can smell the troll, too." And "How'd I miss that. Troll smell is strong."

The mystery of it lingered as I went to the bridge alone later that day. I didn't cross. Just stood at the edge, where the dirt road turned into wooden slats that moved out over the bridge. I might have seen the troll's eye through one of the narrow gaps between the slats, but I couldn't be sure. When I looked more closely, there was nothing there.

I remembered Butter's nervousness and hesitation crossing the bridge. More so than during the day, when there had just been the troll there. Horses are one of the animals that wolves, including atti-wolves, love to eat. Atti-wolves love to eat people, too.

"Thank you," I said aloud. I opened my mouth to say more, but then decided there was nothing more to say. Just, "Thank you." And I returned to the village.

CHAPTER 4

$\mathcal{I}$ didn't have call to cross the bridge for another month. But in that time, as the fall picked up a bite, the weather catching that chilly edge that made heavier clothing feel more comfortable and put that strange autumn light in the air that I loved but always found hard to describe. There was a feel, a look to the light in the fall that *felt* like fall to me. I loved it. But I wasn't looking forward to the winter. I wasn't mad about real cold.

Winter was good for my business, though. Everyone needed their winter jackets repaired, some needed new coats to replace threadbare ones, others needed warmer undergarments and thicker pants and dresses. I was a dressmaker, but I was also the only real tailor in the village, too. Harin Mashis, the previous tailor, had moved to be closer to his daughter's family after his wife passed three years ago. And no one had taken up his business yet. Everyone in the village just came to me.

Which made autumn a very busy work season for me as we prepared for the winter. I didn't mind. I liked being busy. I like my work and keeping my hands active. So the extra hours weren't a problem.

They did keep me from being able to visit with Molly and Angel, though, and I worried. After the first atti-wolf, two more were found. Both dead in the river. Broken necks. One had its head nearly ripped off. No one in our village had died or even seen the atti-wolves before they were found dead.

But three coming down out of the mountains in just a few weeks, when they hadn't any for so many decades, coming down well before deep winter might have naturally driven them down…

We were all worried and the tension was thick in the air around the village.

And I worried about my friend and her newborn in the neighboring village.

That worry finally got the best of me when word reached our village that an atti-wolf had been seen in the area around Molly's village. They didn't have a convenient troll under their bridge. And while no one in my village discussed it, I was certain the troll was the one keeping us safe from the atti-wolf infestation.

Everyone told stories crossing the bridge now. And we left rocks for the troll, rather than letting him give us rocks. I liked to imagine his collection was quite impressive after a month of this. The children even went into the woods and, under parental supervision, to the edge of the river to find the best rocks, all hand pick presents to leave for the troll.

I had been too busy to go to the bridge and tell my own story, but now that my worry for Molly and her family got the best of me, I left my apprentice to watch the shop, selected some lovely stones from the back of my cottage—smooth and gray with little specs of a black sparkling mineral running through them—and headed on foot across the bridge.

I told a story about a brave troll—I was the village tailor after all, so I tailored my story to my audience—who rescued a princess from raiders and was given his own kingdom in return. The troll was a kind and benevolent king and his lands flourished. When I reached the end of the bridge, I set my rocks on the edge, where they would be easy to pick up from under the bridge. I was about to continue on my way, when I spotted a flash of blue and yellow on the opposite side of the bridge.

There, in a small pile, the blue and yellow east mountain rocks the troll had been leaving for stories prior to the atti-wolves. Stones he'd never given me.

I smiled a little and aloud said, "That wasn't necessary. You've done so much for us. But I suppose I finally told a story you liked?"

I might have heard a grunting noise from under the bridge, or it might have been the wind and a conveniently timed splash of water over rocks. The river rushed past a little faster now, but still quite shallow. I'd probably just heard a fish jumping.

Since I didn't want to offend the troll after having only just told a story good enough to earn stones, I collected the pile and put them in the pockets of my walking jacket—a long beaten, soft leather treated with oils to hold out the chill and would keep me relatively dry if it rained—and continued on to Molly's village.

I found Molly's village in an uproar. People running everywhere. Frantic expressions. A panic of shouts and calls and shaking heads. I couldn't get any information from anyone I stopped. They were all in too much of a hurry. The only thing any of them managed to get out was a single warning... Atti-wolf!

People dove into their homes, collected their children

from the streets, locked doors and closed window shutters. The livestock, where possible, were rushed into houses and barns. Pets were scurried inside as well. I didn't go deep into the village, because Molly's house was near the edge, on the road up from my village. But even on the outskirts of town, all this chaotic, frantic activity spoke of panic.

And my panic shot up, too.

I rushed to Molly's house, bumping off people and apologizing. When I reached her cottage, there were a few more people crowding inside than normally visited. People who'd been caught in the neighborhood and needed shelter.

Her husband, Maneesh, stood outside the front door ushering people in. He spotted me and frantically waved his hands. "Get in, get in. They've seen the atti-wolf on the other side of town. We haven't much time."

I only paused long enough to make sure he followed me inside, as the street cleared and no more stragglers remained hunting for shelter. Then I ducked through the door and helped Maneesh bolt it closed.

"Erin!" Molly saw me at the door and pulled me into a hug.

"Everything's okay? Everyone's here?" I looked over her shoulder for Angel. The baby was in the arms of an older woman I didn't know. Angel cooed up at the woman as she made faces for the baby.

There were at least twenty people crammed into the main area of the cottage, sitting around on benches, some sitting on the clean wooden floor, others flitting around making sure the rest were okay. Two people hovered near the shuttered windows at the front of the house and another two at the shuttered windows at the back, keeping watch through thin cracks in the wooden slats.

With the window shutters closed, the cottage was dark but

for the large crackling fire at one side of the room, filling the place with woodsmoke smell which overwhelmed the too-many-people smell. But the heat inside was almost oppressive with so many bodies. Especially after the brisk autumn coolness outside.

I pulled back and met Molly's gaze. "You're okay?"

"Yes, yes. The atti-wolf was spotted at the opposite side of town."

Maneesh joined us and I told them about the dead atti-wolves we'd been finding in the river near us.

"The troll?" Molly asked, her voice low so that only the three of us could hear. "He's been killing them."

"That's what we suspect. Though no one's openly talking about it."

"Wish we had a troll here," Maneesh said, with feeling, then moved away to help some of his panicking neighbors.

Molly pulled me to a seat near the fire. Once we were settled, I showed her the stones. "The troll finally liked one of my stories," I said with a forced grin. "The timing is interesting."

Molly brushed her fingers over the stones, picking up one particularly fine-looking blue stone with a thin line of sparkling blue-gold crystal mineral running through it. "They're very pretty," she said. "I haven't seen so many in one place before. I can see why you were hoping for some. You could probably trade them for useable money up near the castle. There's enough here to set you up for the next year."

I bounced the stones in my palm. "I'd feel ungrateful selling them. They're a gift."

"A gift worth something."

"All gifts are worth something. Even the ones without ordinary value."

Molly smiled a little and shrugged. She held up the blue

rock with the line of glistening mineral. The blue-gold glistened in the light from the fire. "You might well be right."

She handed me back the stone when the room suddenly took on a hushed quiet. We looked around.

Maneesh was standing next to one of the windows with another man who looked like one of his many younger brothers—I think this one was Timor, but I wasn't certain. Maneesh looked grim.

He hushed the room, which was already near silent, with a waving hand and kept his gaze on the street in front of the cottage.

Molly gripped my hand, hard, then let go and motioned the old woman who'd been holding Angel to pass the baby back to her. She cradled her daughter, letting the baby suck on her finger to keep her quiet, as we all watched the front of the house.

The stones in my hands felt heavy and hot, but it took me several breathless moments before I realized they weren't just warm from sitting in my palm. They were getting warmer.

I frowned down at them. The lines of minerals running through the blue and yellow tones were glowing faintly. Just enough I was sure it wasn't the firelight.

They got hot enough they were hard to hold.

A story from my youth, told by one of the village witches, rose from the depths of my memory. Molly had mentioned the tale on one of my recent visits, when I'd first told her about the troll giving out rocks for good stories.

I rose quietly, motioning Molly away when she reached for me. "I'll be right back," I whispered.

At the front, I set three of the rocks on the floor just at the base, where a very thin gap between door and frame let in a cool whisp of air. I was a little afraid the rocks' heat would catch the wood on fire, because they were almost too hot for me to hold now. But despite the glow, the floor seemed unaffected by the heat.

I did the same thing at the back door with three more rocks.

A loud snuffling sound from outside started my heartbeat racing. I went to each window and set a rock on the sill, ending my circuit of the room near Maneesh and his brother. Near his ear, I whispered. "I'm not sure this will help. But it won't hurt."

He nodded, frowning a little as he glanced back out to the street. His sudden gasp shot a powerful rush of adrenaline through me. I took a step away from the window almost instinctively.

A grunt and low sound, a little like a hiss, from just outside had everyone backing away from the front of the house, crowding farther into the middle of the room. Maneesh went to Molly and wrapped his arms around her and Angel. I stood close to them. We all watched the front door.

The handle rattled. A number of people gasped and a worried moment of chatter followed, hushed only at a harsh word from Maneesh.

The door handle rattled again. The gasps and worried sounds were more restrained this time, but one of the women burst into tears.

I glanced down at the stones on the floor just inside the door and realized they were glowing now. Not just the lines of minerals running through them, but fully glowing, bright cobalt blue and daisy yellow like mini-stars dropped to the earth.

The door handle rattled again, and then a howl went up, so piercing I had to cover my ears. A howl that sounded like pain.

And then silence. For a long long moment. Nothing but silence.

CHAPTER 5

e all sat in that silence for a long time before anyone risked going to a window to check what was happening outside. The door didn't rattle again. And the glowing rocks faded back to their normal colors.

When Maneesh finally did go to check on the street, my nerves were stretched so tight I couldn't keep my hands still. I kept dipping them into my pockets and pulling them out again, restlessness and nerves putting me into near constant motion where just moments ago I'd been still as a waiting statue.

Maneesh straightened suddenly away from the window, which made a few of us gasp. Then he threw open the shutter. A brief protest rose, but he cut it off with a hand gesture. Frowning, he looked at me, at the stones, then at Molly and the baby.

Finally, he signaled to his brother. When Timor joined him, he motioned to the street. They exchanged a look. Then both looked at me.

"What?" I looked between them. "What's happened?"

"The atti-wolf..." Maneesh gestured outside. "It's laying in the street. Not moving."

"A trick?" one of the villagers asked.

"Never heard of them using tricks to hunt," another said.

"Careful," Molly said, her tone a little frantic. "Don't go outside yet."

I went to the window, unable to resist seeing what Maneesh was seeing.

Outside, in the middle of the road, beyond Molly's front garden, lay the atti-wolf. This one was the size of a cow. We were looking at the beast's stomach and paws, so I couldn't tell if its neck was broken or not. But its ribs weren't rising and falling with breath.

There was a lot of debate and more time passed before Maneesh finally opened the door and, with several of the villagers, went outside to check on the atti-wolf. From across the street, more doors opened, and more people came out. Hesitantly. Ready to dash back inside if necessary.

It wasn't necessary.

Once close enough to see the wolf clearly, it became obvious...

The beast's neck was broken, its head nearly ripped off.

It was dead.

* * *

Before I returned home later that afternoon, I insisted Molly and her family keep the blue and yellow stones, despite their protests. I did let Maneesh and two of his brothers escort me back to the bridge, though. They brought their hunting bows and we all kept an eye on the surrounding forest.

At the bridge, before crossing, I said aloud, "Thank you

for the stones. I've left them with my friend. I hope that's okay."

There was a little grunt from beneath the bridge. Timor took a step back, startled by the sound. I smiled a little and waved the men goodbye as I crossed the wooden slates, heading home.

I told another brave troll story, because I felt the troll deserved one. This of a troll who saves an entire village with his bravery.

There were no blue or yellow stones waiting for me at the other end of the bridge this time. But there was one of the gray rocks with black mineral lines that I'd left earlier for the troll. The black mineral line wasn't black anymore though. It was more purple. I picked the rock up and angled it in the dying evening light. The purple glittered, and the rock felt warm in my palm. Not hot, but comfortingly warm.

I smiled. "Thank you."

I took the rock home and set it by my front door after I'd closed myself in for the night.

We're still not sure what killed the atti-wolf in Molly's village. If it was the troll come all that way, or if it was some magic in the rocks. And really, it didn't matter. For the winter, all the rocks the troll had given us were spread around both our village and Molly's. The troll gave us more for more stories—even me—and we ensured every house in the two villages had something to put at their front door.

By the end of the winter, we stopped seeing any signs of atti-wolves, dead or alive. When the river waters rose that spring, the smell of troll vanished for a short time. Which left all of us upset and sad. Like a member of the village had moved away. But as the river levels dropped, later in spring, the smell returned to our bridge.

So the stories continued, each a toll paid as we crossed

the bridge, each story thanked in whatever way the troll saw fit.

There weren't a lot of trolls in our area. Not every village was lucky enough to have a troll under the bridge. But we were. For many many years.

And whenever I returned to my village from some travel, that distinctive ripe troll smell, a little like burnt wood and badger, welcomed me back.

Welcomed me home.

CARY AT THE CROSSROADS

A CARY REDMOND NOVELLA

CHAPTER 1

Cary Redmond tossed the tennis ball to Fred, her mundane collie-terrier mix, and watched him tear across her small backyard, charging the trees at the back of the yard and bouncing off the wooden fence when the ball did, changing directions to chase it into the grass. Once he caught it, he charged back at top speed, leaping up the two short stairs to the deck as if they didn't exist, a blur of white and light brown fur.

Pickles, her basset hound who was actually a foo lion, raised her head from the spot next to Cary's hip where they sat at the edge of the top step, gave Fred a deep *woof* that probably meant "be careful," then lowered her head, her jowls and ears spreading wide on the wooden deck, and closed her eyes.

Buck, the golden Labrador who was a demon dog—not hellhound, he hated that name—didn't even raise his head or so much as open his eyes from where he snoozed farther down the deck next to Pickles. To be fair, he'd already had to move once because Fred kept careening into him, so he'd earned his nap.

The early October sun was warm and bright, the clouds few and white and fluffy. After days of rain, this was the first sunny morning they'd had in a while, and everyone was very excited to take advantage of that. But most especially Fred.

Cary grinned at her little dog pack, wondered idly if Scratchy the stray cat might make an appearance, and tossed the soggy green tennis ball Fred dropped at her hip across the yard again. She chuckled as Fred clattered down the stairs—why he didn't leap down the way he leapt up, she wasn't sure—and tore across the grass to the back fence. Again.

She needed to mow her lawn. The grass was getting long, and it was damp from all the rain, which meant Fred was going to need toweling off when they went back inside for coffee and snacks, seeing as how everyone was earning a midmorning snack by soaking up the sunshine.

A noise from the front of the house, the doorbell buzzing nonstop, like someone had put a finger to it and wasn't taking that irritating finger off the bell, made her sigh. Guess it was time to get to work.

"Gotta go inside," she said to the dogs. "That'll be Jaxer. And he's being his usual irritating self."

She pushed up from the step as Fred came racing back, leaving his soggy tennis ball in the yard in favor of mudroom treats. She considered making him go get it, but Jaxer hadn't taken his finger off the bell yet, so she really needed to get inside. She'd get the ball later.

Inside, she the mudroom, she dropped a towel on Fred and gave him a quick dry, then gave all three dogs a treat from the treat jar on the shelf where she kept her hats and gloves, and finally went through the kitchen to the living room to get the door. She had no idea her doorbell could make that noise so continuously. It was both irritating and mildly amazing that Jaxer could get the sound to just go on and on and on.

She jerked the door open to his grinning expression and shook her head. "I was in back. I needed a minute. You could have just…stopped when you knew I knew you were here."

"Where's the fun in that?" he said as he dropped a kiss on her cheek then skirted around her and walked into her living room like he lived there.

She actually had no idea where her faery mentor lived. Paris? China? She was pretty sure it wasn't inside Faery—something complicated to do with his past and the English and Irish Fae courts, something he'd never explained to her—but other than that, she had no idea. He passed through Faery a lot. She knew that much. But other than that, she had no idea what he did or where he went when he wasn't pestering her. He just showed up when she had a job to do or training of some kind he wanted to impose on her, which was admittedly less often these days.

And actually, her bosses, the North American Fae who created Protectors, were usually the ones who showed up at all hours, materializing in her home without more than a tingling along her spine as warning, with the jobs. Jaxer mostly showed up afterward, when things were going wrong or she needed help.

Since she wasn't currently on a job having just rescued three separate people from three different illusion spells across three different parts of the city over the last three days, Jaxer showing up today was…suspicious.

"What's going on?" she asked, eyes narrowed as she closed the door and followed him into the living room.

He sprawled on the big couch, looking his usual ridiculously handsome self. He was dressed in linen trousers and silk shirt, open just enough at the collar to reveal the muscles on his chest. The deep blue color of his shirt brought out the blue in his blue-green eyes. His blond hair was short and artfully mussed, which made her want to roll her eyes. Especially since her hair was really mussed from the wind and a lazy morning playing with the dogs, and she was dressed in jeans covered in dog hair and one muddy, Fred-sized paw print.

It really was ridiculous how handsome he was. She knew he used his glamour—his most powerful magic—to alter the way he looked to humans, but she'd always suspected he actually dampened his gorgeousness instead of enhanced it. He was vain enough to enhance it. But she got the feeling, if he dropped the glamour and showed the mundane world his real self, he'd probably blind people.

Fortunately, she was basically immune to handsomeness at this stage—thanks, in fact, to Jaxer always introducing her to gorgeous men who turned out to be preternatural Trouble and who often wanted to kill her—or she'd have developed a mean crush on her mentor. As it was, he'd become her friend. A close friend who she, mostly, trusted with her life. He'd been with her since she'd become a magical Protector, a job her bosses had basically tricked her into, a ruse which Jaxer held some blame for as well. But he'd taught her what she needed to know in this weird magical world, a world she'd known nothing about before becoming a Protector... wow, almost seven years ago now. And since she'd managed to survive for those almost seven years, she was grateful to him.

Most of the time.

This was not going to be one of those times, though. She knew it in her gut. This was going to be one of those times she wanted to throw Fred's soggy green tennis ball at his face.

"So, you know how there's been a bit of trouble with illusion spells lately?"

She snorted. "Three days in a row trouble? Yes. I vividly remember." Because she'd had to spend a lot of time in the rain over the last three days. And getting soaked to the skin while wearing jeans three days in a row is hard to forget. Jeans *rub* when they get wet. Chafe. And her thighs were not happy with the chaffing.

Jaxer spread his hands and said, "That was…part of something bigger, I'm afraid."

"Why aren't the Nags here sending me out to save someone, then? What bigger? What does bigger mean?"

"First, Wisat and Liruk aren't here because they're trying to figure out what the bigger is. Second, we don't know for sure what the bigger is."

"Well that's going to complicate me protecting someone, isn't it?" And the fact that her bosses did not know what the "bigger" thing was was definitely an issue. "Is there even someone for me to protect yet?"

"There are hints," he said. "But they haven't been able to pin it down."

Her bosses, Wisat and Liruk, figured out where to send her through premonitions, instinct, and good old-fashioned research. They were, in generally, very good at it. But the problem with premonitions was they weren't predictable or consistent. As far as she knew, neither Wisat nor Liruk could force those premonitions.

More often than not, her bosses—who she called Nags because they were—got the premonitions in time to send her out to save someone, or put her on the right track to saving people. But not always. If they always got it right, no one would ever be hurt again. Well, within reason. There was only one of her for all of Portland. She couldn't be in two places at once. And Portland was a large enough city to complicate her protecting every single person, even if she could be in two places at once. And even if she *could* protect the entire city all at once—she was pretty sure she couldn't— she couldn't do it indefinitely.

So she'd had to accept from the beginning that the only thing she could do was the best she could do. And accept she couldn't save everyone. She answered the tingling call that indicated her brand of help was needed when that happened spontaneously. And she went were her bosses sent her to save people.

But she lived in constant fear that she wasn't enough, that she wasn't *actually* supposed to be doing this job, and one day she'd fail and someone would die. So far, that hadn't happened. But knowing it could, sometimes left her edgy and more terrified than the dangers she faced doing her job.

Right now, she was very worried about not knowing where to go. That left open the possibility that someone who needed her would get hurt. Or worse. Knowing she was needed *somewhere* but they weren't sure where yet was scary.

"How do you guys know the illusion traps were leading to something bigger?" she asked.

The dogs came in from the mudroom, through the kitchen, and went right for their doggie beds underneath the big bay window in her living room, a window that looked out onto the bright sunny day spilling into her small backyard. The sun seemed to mock her now, though. Clouds would be more in keeping with her current mood and the worry that had started to churn in her gut.

"Threes," Jaxer said with a shrug.

Cary sighed and closed her eyes. She should have realized. "Three days. Three people. Three spells." The preternatural world liked threes. Things were stronger in threes. Things happened in threes. Things got worse in threes.

"The illusion spells are from a faery of some kind," Jaxer said. "We do know that."

"Someone like you is doing this?"

"A faery," he said, his mouth flattening.

Okay. So she'd apparently insulted him. Guess he didn't like being of the same species as the bad guy. She was used to it now. Lot of human bad guys out there.

"What does that mean?" she asked, her hands on her hips. She couldn't sit with the anxiety and antsiness prickling across her nerves so she stayed standing.

"What it means is, we're due a bit of faery chaos soon. But we're not sure to what end."

His Irish accent, faint and subtle most of the time, had gotten stronger as he spoke. He was definitely more upset about what was happening than he let on.

"So you're just here to worry me about this? There's nothing for me to do yet?"

"Oh, no, there's something for you to do."

"Well why didn't you just say so?" She huffed. "What?"

"We're going to the crossroads."

"The crossroads?"

Why did a simple, generic word sound so...deadly?

CHAPTER 2

"This is the crossroads, huh?" Cary wrapped her leather jacket tighter around her and stomped her booted feet to get the chill out.

The "crossroads" as it turned out was a couple of country lanes intersecting in what felt like a very random part of the farming fields south of the city. There were a lot of these "crossroads" all over the place. There were a lot of "crossroads" inside Portland for that matter.

So what the hell made this one special?

Although the day had been warm and sunny, now that night had fallen, early autumn cold was creeping in. The air was damp but the night was clear, and somehow that clear black sky overhead seemed to make everything feel colder.

Actually, it was a *lot* colder than it really should have been. Chilly at this time of year, sure. But see-her-breath-cold? Not so much.

"And why the hell is it freezing?" she demanded of her mentor.

The Fae in question stood seemingly unaffected by the cold next to her in his open silk shirt and linen trousers, but his hair ruffled with the breeze and she could see his breath, too.

"This is not a natural cold," Jaxer said. "It's the crossroads."

"Okay, I know I'm supposed to be studying all this and should probably know already, but…what?"

He glanced at her with his patient teacher expression and she narrowed her eyes. That expression usually made her want to smack him in the face with a pillow because it meant he was about to patiently tell her something she should have already learned in all the years of studying. But there was just so damned much to *learn*. It was impossible to learn it all. The preternatural world was immense and complicated and there was a lot more there there than most humans ever suspected.

"It's a Fae thing," he said.

"A Fae thing?"

"A Fae thing. The crossroads are places where the Fae travel and interact with the human world. And meeting Fae at a crossroads is usually bad for any human. They end up drained, dead, exhausted, pulled into Faery, enthralled, all sorts of things."

"That all sounds bad. Why is it cold?"

"The Fae are coming."

"Which ones and why?" She huffed out a breath, scowled at the puff of fog. Then blinked. Speaking of fog.

The ground, which had just a few moments ago been dirt bracketed by grassy fields, was now covered in a low swirl of fog. If she didn't look down, or out across the fields, she might not notice. But the creep of cold fingers spread over her ankles and made her want to stomp her feet to shake loose the feeling.

"Is this fog dangerous?" she asked, giving it a look.

The problem with her Protector powers was that they only activated when she was protecting someone. When she got between bad guys and good guys, those powers flowed into her—nothing she actively did, the magic was just there when she needed it—and her Protector shield went up, and both herself and her charge were safe. And she could keep her charge, and by extension herself, safe like that until the end times. As far as she could tell, the shield never wore out or gave out. So long as there was danger to *someone else*, the shield stayed up.

The fine print, though, was that if she didn't have anyone to protect, she was just an ordinary human woman. Had always been just an ordinary human woman. And the magic didn't come up to protect *her*. She was just as vulnerable as any other human. She could be mugged. She could be killed. So long as the bad guys were aiming for her and no one else, she could be harmed. Or even if she was in a car crash with no one else in danger, or…she didn't know, the ground opened up during an earthquake and no one else was around, or something… Any sort of natural accident could kill her, too, if there weren't any other people around for her to protect.

She couldn't protect herself. Not using her Protector magic.

So if this fog was dangerous to humans, she really needed someone to protect in order to be safe herself. Jaxer might work—she'd done that before, protected him so they'd both be safe—but he was Fae so this cold fog might not even affect him.

"You'll be fine," Jaxer said, his attention on the roads and not on her or the ground.

"Why don't I believe you?" She continued to scowl at the fog. "What are we waiting for?"

"The person you'll need to protect from the Riders."

"The Riders?"

That patient look again. She gave him a deadpan stare.

"Sorry, but this is pretty basic Fae mythology."

"For North America? The Riders are supposed to be an Irish thing."

His eyebrows shot up. "So. You have studied."

"Stop. You sound like Liruk. But you, I will pelt with rocks."

He grinned. It was a real shit-eater grin, as her dad would say. "The Riders are part of the Irish Fae. There are Riders in parts of Scotland and Wales, too. But most of the Riders stick to the Tuatha de Dana court."

"So what are they doing here?"

He frowned and turned back to the road. "Good question."

She glanced down at the fog. It was higher now, covering her feet. "I need someone to protect," she murmured. Especially if the Riders were really the issue.

The Riders were a hoard of High Fae who took to the road on their horses, racing through the night. If an unlucky human encountered the Race, they usually ended up either pulled into it—to waste away to nothing in Faery—or died from the shock of it. Once Christianity hit Ireland, the Riders were thought to be demonic in nature, but demons were something very different to Fae. Fae were just as dangerous. They just weren't demons.

The problem, as Cary saw it, was that the Riders were known to look and feel...ghostly. And she was terrified of ghosts. To her core terrified. The Riders were *not* ghosts, which was an important distinction and one she needed to keep reminding herself of, but they could *look* like ghosts.

Apparently, their approach came with all the freezing air

that could warn of a ghost, too. That was the part she hadn't remembered from her readings. The cold.

She should have remembered the cold.

"So how have all the illusion traps triggered in the last three days gotten us here? And who am I here to protect? And why are the Riders here in the US? And what's going on?" She was trying not to panic about ghosts, but it was there in the background, waiting for her to forget these weren't ghosts.

"The three days of three illusion traps triggered by three humans is what has called the Riders. Those were set by someone for the specific purpose of bringing the Race this way. The Race being here is because this is where the illusion traps triggered. What's going on? I have no idea. Neither did Wisat or Liruk."

"You all are Fae and you don't know why someone might bring the Riders here?"

"Premonitions are not omnipotent."

She'd heard that before. She made a face. The why's of all this didn't matter to her being able to do her job. She was just curious. And hated not knowing why something was happening.

"You haven't told me the who yet, though. The who seems to be an important point here."

"The who is the real problem," Jaxer murmured.

"Because you don't know who the who is?"

"Because whoever has done this is in as much danger as they're likely to cause."

"I'm going to have to protect a bad guy, aren't I?" She hated doing that. It was necessary sometimes. If some idiot got themselves into trouble trying to do something nefarious or greedy, then ended up being the victims of their own hubris, she had to jump in a protect them from themselves.

Talk about *irritating*. She hated when she had to protect bad guys.

"Not sure," Jaxer said. "Not sure if the person we're waiting for is the one who called the Riders or just the focal point of the Race."

"That made no sense to me. You know that, right?"

"I'll explain when I understand better."

"Oh good." Her sarcasm earned her a look. She grinned at him, because poking at him when he was annoying her was fun.

She glanced down at the fog again. "Does this affect you? Are you in any danger?"

He flicked a look to the fog, then away to the road again. "No. It's…Faery creeping into the human realm. I'm fine."

"That's not great for me. You know that, right?"

"We have until midnight. You'll have someone to protect before the Riders arrive."

She stared down the road. It was only ten minutes to midnight. The road was empty of humans for her to keep safe. And at the very edge of her hearing, she was picking up the sounds of…hooves pounding the ground.

Her heartbeat started to hammer and she took a step closer to Jaxer.

"You sure about that?" she murmured. Because she wasn't.

And the fog was getting thicker.

CHAPTER 3

$\mathcal{A}$ clock started ticking down in Cary's head as the faint sound of hooves pounding against the dirt road got just a little louder. The air around her dropped another few degrees in temperature. She shoved her hands into her jacket pockets to keep them warm, but her leather jacket could only do so much against the preternatural cold. She'd have to ask Marianne, her weaver best friend who'd made this jacket for her—a jacket with magical pockets—if she could add a handwarmer spell to the side pockets. Hadn't occurred to her before that that was something she might need.

It was occurring to her now.

The fog covering the ground had blotted out the dirt roads and the surrounding grassy fields. She could no longer see the actual crossroads anymore, just the red stop sign rising above the fog to one side of the intersection. There were trees somewhere out in the fields that just looked like shadows now. And a scent of…sulfur was creeping in with the fog.

"I thought the Riders were Fae and not demonic for real,"

she whispered to Jaxer, whose full attention was on the road. "I thought that demonic thing was just something the Christians came up with."

"They are Fae. They are not demons."

"Then why am I smelling sulfur?"

"Because a being doesn't need to be a demon to exhibit demonic characteristics."

"Since when?" she asked, her voice rising. But the sound cracked in the quiet like a whip and made her jump. Heat flooded her cheeks. She'd just startled at the sound of her own voice. And Jaxer was here to witness it. How embarrassing.

The sound of hooves pounding dirt got closer. Beyond the approaching horses, though, there was no other sound. No shouts or whoops or calls. No urging the horses on. Cary couldn't even see a glow or hint of which direction the Riders were coming from.

Just the sound of horses approaching fast. And the scent of sulfur.

"I'm still without anyone to protect," she murmured to Jaxer, moving even closer to him, so her shoulder touched his. "This is bad. I shouldn't be here if there's no one to protect."

"You can protect me."

"*You're* not in danger. Remember. These are Fae and you're a faery and this is a little bit of Faery creeping out into the human world so you're safe. We just established that."

He wasn't looking at her, he was watching a spot along the road, and she found herself staring in that same direction even though she couldn't tell if that was the direction the Riders were coming from or something else. There were no cars on the road. Hers was parked behind them, pulled off to the side, out of the way in case cars came by, but none had. Jaxer had met her here, preferring to get here by his own method. He didn't have a strong iron allergy like many Fae, but still a mild allergy. He could be inside houses and buildings. He could even touch wrought iron. But he wasn't comfortable inside cars so he never rode in them.

The thought of the iron allergy had her glancing back to her car, the entire lower half of it covered in fog. "Would I be safe inside the car?" she asked.

"There's supposed to be someone here," he muttered. "The Riders wouldn't be here if someone hadn't summoned them to this crossroads."

"Maybe they forgot? Fell asleep? Got the location wrong? Maybe they, whoever they are, didn't know what they were doing and all this is an accident and that's why they're not here?"

He shook his head but she couldn't tell what the gesture meant.

The sound of the running horses was almost on them.

The ticking clock in Cary's head had nearly reached midnight even if she wasn't looking at a clock. She didn't need to know it was only a minute to midnight to know it was almost midnight.

"Should I...wait in the car?" She started backing toward her sturdy Prius even as the pounding hooves got louder. So loud she was a little amazed she couldn't see anything yet.

"Yeah," Jaxer said after an excruciating moment. "Yeah. Get into the car. This is... Something's wrong here."

She was tempted to say, "You think?!" but she was too busy hurrying back to her car, trying not to trip since she couldn't see what she was stepping on through the thick ground fog anymore.

She reached the car, was about to pull the door open, when she felt a wash of heat along her spine.

Given how cold it was, that heat was strong enough to make her turn.

She should have gotten into the car first.

A huge horse, something roughly the size of a Clydesdale, but sleek like an Arabian, stood in front of Jaxer, its hair, tail, and mane all silky white but its nostrils and eyes glowed red. It snorted and steam came from its nose to mingle with the fog covering the ground, which was up to Cary's calf now.

On the horse's back sat a Rider. Cary had only seen artist illustrations of Riders in the books in her secret attic library. No one had ever gotten a picture of one. Hell, only a few people had survived to describe them. The artists had to work off those descriptions so their work was just an approximation.

The approximation did not do justice to the actual Rider in real life.

High Fae, ethereal, large like their horse. Human shaped in that they had a head at the top, legs—only two—arms—again only two—and a torso. But the being on top of that stomping, snorting white horse could not be described as human even on a bad day. They were also white, wearing a flowing gown of gossamer white material that flowed around them in a breeze Cary couldn't feel. Their hair was long and white and decorated with little red flowers that looked like rubies. Or blood drops. A face cut in sharp, narrow angles, so that everything was a little longer or sharper or closer together than would happen on a human face. And their white skin—not just Cary's human white woman white, but no color, not even a blush-in-the-cheeks white—glowed the way their horse glowed. Lit from within.

It was actually hard to tell where the Rider ended and the

horse began. They almost looked like a single creature. Not, like, a centaur or something. But like the Rider always sat atop their horse, and the horse always carried their Rider, and the two did this forever.

And maybe they did. From her readings, Cary understood the Race was eternal—that was kind of the problem for humans who got sucked into the Race—and the Riders were their own sort of court. Though they were from Ireland, and technically of the Tuatha de Dana, they weren't, apparently, beholden to Danu's court.

All this went through her head as she just stood there beside her car staring. One hand on the door handle, her body frozen in place, unable to do more than stare. Her breath puffed out of her in smoke that wasn't unlike the horse's. The scent of sulfur had changed to something earthy, like musk and damp soil, a combination that was a lot nicer than the sulfur. So much so, she wanted to let go of the door handle and wander closer to the Rider so she could parse out that better smell. Were there pine needles in there? Gosh she liked the smell of pine needles. Reminded her of Christmas trees.

That Rider was more attractive than she'd realized, too. Not horrific and terrifying and ghostly after all, but... surprisingly handsome. Sexy even? Were they the one who smelled like pine needles and earth? Or was that the horse? She hadn't ridden a horse in years and years. Not since she was a kid. But she liked horses. That horse might be fun to ride.

There was a very good reason she shouldn't try to ride one of those horses, though, wasn't there? Something to do with the way the horse's eyes glowed red...

She tried to blink, but she couldn't seem to do that because it would mean looking away from the Rider and she didn't want to stop looking at the Rider.

The Fae glanced around the countryside. Behind them, blurs of movement, like streaks of white, flowed past, but no solid shape formed inside the fog. Cary got the impression of a horse nose here, a glowing eye there, a stretching horse leg. The strike of hooves on packed earth still sounded, loud now even though most of the Riders weren't visible.

"Where are we?" the Rider asked Jaxer, their voice deep and wispy at once. A discordant combination that did nothing to break through Cary's fascination with the being. "This is not our usual route."

"I would ask you the same," Jaxer said.

Cary almost did blink at the sound of his voice, and her head turned just a little, as if she'd look away from the Rider to look at her mentor. He sounded different. His voice was… regal? Deep and the Irish burr now clipped and more pronounced. From the side of her eye, she'd swear he looked different, too. But she couldn't seem to look away from the Rider long enough to check.

Her hand tightened on the car door handle. The steel felt hot to the touch, like it was burning her. But also that felt good. Shocking. Grounding.

Why did she need to keep holding the door handle? Why did she need to look away from the Rider? There was a reason. What was the reason…?

"We race," the Rider said. "The Race is eternal. We were…called here."

"Yes," Jaxer said. "But you should not be. You are in North America, in the human realm."

"We touch on the human realm always at the crossroads. This is a crossroads."

"And it is not one you should be at. You were called here. Do you know by whom?"

Wow, Jaxer sounded formal. By whom? Yeah, yeah, that

was correct grammar and all, but also sounded *very* formal from Jaxer.

Cary's lashes flickered. Not quite a blink. Under the alluring smell of pine needles and earth, a sharper scent crept in. Something sour…

The horse snorted and stomped its hoof into the fog. Sparks rose up around the horse's leg.

"We have been summoned to this crossroads," the Rider said. "It was not by you, Jaxer of the Dana?"

"It was not," Jaxer said.

Jaxer of the Dana? What? Oh, that begged all kinds of questions, didn't it?

Cary's hand tightened on the door handle.

"Will you ride with us anyway? The Race would welcome you."

Oh! No, wait. Jaxer couldn't join the Race. He'd leave. She'd lose her mentor. She needed a mentor still. There was still so much to learn. She had people to save. And she needed his help to do that.

Wait. She had people to save? What was that about?

She blinked.

She was a Protector. She saved people from bad guys. Jaxer was her mentor. And whatever the hell had just happened to her was not cool.

She snapped open the car door and reached inside, scrambling through the papers in her glove compartment. Had to be in here somewhere… Her dad insisted…

Ah ha! She plucked out the flashlight. An old one her dad had given her when she went off to college. Told her to keep one in her car, one in her house. Always keep the batteries new. Unlike most of the newer flashlights, her old ones from her dad weren't housed in soft plastic casings. This was one of those heavy-duty lights, solid enough to be a weapon if she needed it. And while the grip was covered in rubber, the bulk of the flashlight was metal. Steel.

Steel was an alloy made with iron.

She hefted the old flashlight, grateful she'd never upgraded to a plastic one, and carried it in front of her like a talisman as she hurried to Jaxer.

She could not let him get sucked into the Race.

Cary, automatically and without thinking about the consequences, scooted between Jaxer and the white glowing horse with the red glowing eyes and its white glowing Rider who had just moments ago been so fascinating to her she couldn't look away. Probably getting even closer to that lure was a bad idea. But Jaxer might be talked into joining the Race, getting on a horse and charging away.

And Cary was not about to let that happen.

She held her big flashlight up in front of her, like it would really do something against the High Fae, and was more than a little surprised when the horse danced away from the steel cylinder in her hand, taking itself and its rider a yard away instead of standing right up next to Jaxer.

That was good. Better.

"What are you doing?" Jaxer asked in her ear.

His voice sounded normal now. Like the Jaxer she'd known for years. That was good, too.

"You were going to join the Race. Not gonna let that happen."

"I wasn't." A pause. Then, "But thank you for jumping in."

"Am I protecting you from anything?" she whispered even though that was probably pointless. She was sure the Rider could hear her. But she didn't tell people what she was or what she did. Especially dangerous beings like a High Fae. If dangerous beings knew what she was, they could figure out how to get around her Protector shield to kill her.

Except...

Well, she was pretty sure she didn't have a Protector shield right now.

"Not technically," Jaxer murmured. "But the flashlight is working. Inspired."

"Is it hurting you?"

"Not enough for you to put it away."

"Who are you, human?" the Rider demanded, their voice deeper and harsher than it had been when speaking with Jaxer.

And, Cary realized, there was no lure in it. No attempt to seduce her into joining the Race. Was it something she said?

She smiled up at the glowing being. "No one. Just a concerned citizen."

The Rider scowled at her. It was a scary scowl.

She raised the flashlight a little more and said, "You got called here off your usual route. Gotta mean something, right?" Then to Jaxer said, "What the hell does it mean? What's happening? If they don't know why they're here... What is going on?"

"Good question."

Cary frowned at the fog around the Rider, her gaze dancing to the blur of the Race behind them. The Riders didn't...do anything but suck humans into the Race. They didn't give humans anything. They didn't offer rewards or riches. They were just the Riders, and if a human was unlucky enough to encounter them, the human got to run until they died. Yay, with a heavy emphasis on the sarcasm.

So why lure them to this particular crossroads where…if she and Jaxer hadn't shown up, they would not have encountered anyone at all?

"The one who set the illusion spells," she said, "that was obviously the one who summoned the Riders, but…why if they're not even here?"

That was the weird part. She supposed it could have still been an accident, but that seemed like a pretty big accident. More likely had to be someone who knew what they were doing, right. So…where were they?

"Someone who knew enough to set a string of illusion spells, in threes, to trap three different humans…" She muttered aloud, trying to work through it. Was there something about the humans she'd saved?

She hadn't thought so at the time. They'd seemed like random people inadvertently caught in the traps. A younger woman who worked at the big bookstore in town. An older man who'd retired from his accountancy business last year, but said he still occasionally did taxes for people. And a woman around Cary's age who'd just been out walking her dog—the dog's name had been Ambrose and he was an adorable and friendly poodle.

Even as she thought back on them, there was nothing about the three people that screamed of them having a connection. No one said, "Hey, this just happened to a friend of mine?" Or anything to indicate this wasn't their first confrontation with magic. They'd all been ordinary humans. No witches or wizards among them. No shifters. No Fae. They hadn't been in the same neighborhood when triggering the spells even.

In fact, the spells had been at very different places in the city. She'd have to look at a map to see if there was a pattern, though, because she hadn't been looking out for one before this moment. There probably was one, though, because this was magic and the Fae. But even Jaxer and her bosses hadn't spotted a pattern. Outside of the threes.

Threes…

With the Fae, there were always numbers that were significant. Things happening in threes. Sometimes there was that whole year and a day thing, though that tended to be for geasa and curses and things.

But this was a threes thing, wasn't it. Three illusion spells, triggered by three random humans, in three different locations, over three days. Which brought the Riders to a crossroads. At midnight.

"Wait." She half-turned to face Jaxer while still keeping the flashlight in front of her like it was a shield. The steel felt so cold against her palm it almost burned and she realized she was puffing smoke with each breath. The air was absolutely freezing. But she barely noticed it now. "This is just the first night of the Riders. Will they come back this way again? There're all these threes, right? Maybe it's the third night when something is supposed to happen?"

Jaxer scowled, his gaze jumping from the Rider and their snorting horse, back to Cary. Then to the Rider, Jaxer said, "The Race continues?"

"Of course."

"And will pass this way again?"

The Rider was silent for several long moments, before saying… "The Race will pass here again. Twice more."

"Ah ha!" Cary said, then cringed because her voice had been overly loud. "So I bet we're waiting on whatever's going to happen until the third night."

Jaxer frowned. "The Riders are here now, though."

"And are coming back two more times, right? So, if whatever is supposed to happen, happened tonight, there'd be, what two more nights to undue it? Or something. I don't know. But it's threes and threes are important."

She huffed. She really didn't know for sure what she was talking about. Only knew she was onto something with the threes. And that she and Jaxer were early.

The Rider glanced over their shoulder to the stream of movement behind them that Cary could only barely see. "If you are not joining us tonight, Jaxer of the Dana, we will continue." The Rider glanced back at them, the horse reared, and then they leapt forward, vanishing into the stream of movement.

The sounds of the horses' hooves hitting dirt started to fade, the scent of churned earth and sulfur faded with it.

Cary blinked a few times as silence descended over the fields, the fog sank back into the ground, the night breeze blew the scents of ordinary grass and dirt past her face. The temperature rose significantly. The crossroads were quiet. Everything back to normal.

"Well that was weird," she said.

"And we have two more nights of this," Jaxer said.

"Wait, what?" She finally turned to face him, moving the flashlight behind her back so she wouldn't accidentally hit him with it.

"We can't risk the Riders passing this way and some innocent human stumbling on them. We'll have to be here both of the remaining nights."

That made sense, but... "Since I didn't have to protect you, I nearly got sucked into the lure of the Race tonight. I think the only thing keeping me from succumbing was the fact I was holding a steel door handle."

She didn't mention that the thing that had snapped her out of the thrall was the fear of Jaxer running off back to Faery and leaving her to navigate this Protector business on her own. Even after nearly seven years, she didn't feel like she could survive this world without his help. But if she admitted that out loud, he'd get all smug and she'd get annoyed and they didn't have time for his smugness or her annoyance.

"Without someone to protect, this is dangerous for me."

He nodded. "Tomorrow, you stay in the car."

"And you?"

"I'll keep my interaction with the Riders to a minimum. And I promise not to join the Race. Fair enough?"

"It'll have to be. Any idea what we're in for on the third night?"

"No."

Oh boy.

Night two went similarly to night one. Cary parked at the crossroads. Fog filled the area and the temperature dropped sharply. The sound of hooves pounding the dirt heralded the Riders' arrival. Jaxer had a very brief conversation with one of the Fae, who seemed to be the same one from the night before, but Cary couldn't tell for sure, because unlike night one, she knew better and stayed inside her car on night two.

That was the big difference. She stayed inside the car. They had the engine off, so she still felt the cold biting into her bones. But she was surrounded by iron bearing steel, she had her trusty steel flashlight in her lap, and for night two, she'd brought a bunch of metal things that had enough cumulative iron to make even Jaxer wince.

She wore a string of cheap silverware that was more steel than silver on a leather strap around her neck—leather because she could use it to wrap around the handles and because it was what she had on hand. She had gloves to which she'd glued steel bolts from her—not often used but her dad also insisted and so it was very well stocked—tool box, which served the dual purpose of being an anti-Fae device and kept her hands warm when the temperature dropped.

She'd also stuck various screwdrivers and pliers into her jacket, which were not only made with plenty of iron in the steel but could also serve as actual physical weapons if she needed them. Not that she was any good at hand-to-hand fighting using things like screwdrivers and pliers. Despite her other best friend Lucy's efforts, Cary was very inconsistent with her martial arts training. Inconsistent meaning she only actually went to the dojo without making an excuse to avoid it about once a month. Okay, once every other month. But she went. Just, not often enough to get any good at hand-to-hand.

In her defense, she didn't actually need to learn to do that kind of thing for real, because if she needed fighting skills to protect someone, the Protector magic would give her the skills. The magic gave her what she needed to keep her charges safe. The thing was, mostly all she needed was to just stand in place and let the bad guys wear themselves out against her shield.

On night two at the crossroads, however, she wasn't anticipating having anyone to protect. Thus, all the iron laced into her clothing and hanging off her person.

She wasn't disappointed. After the brief conversation with Jaxer, the Rider's horse reared and launched back into the Race, which Cary still only saw as a blur even from the safety of her car. The fog receded. The sound of hooves pounding the dirt died away.

And it was just her sitting in her car, clanging with her ridiculous but effective homemade protection against the Fae, and Jaxer standing at the crossroads, staring off in the direction the Race had gone.

Cary counted to ten before climbing out of the car. She

wasn't sure why. Just felt like she should give the Riders a count of ten to be well and truly gone. She clattered and clanged to within a few feet of Jaxer and then stopped because she didn't want to make him sick with all the iron.

He gave her a raised-brow look that might have been a smirk on a different night but tonight he mostly looked distracted. And frustrated.

"So definitely gonna need to come back tomorrow night," she said, looking around at the empty grass fields and lightless dirt roads. It was just past midnight, and the natural temperature was chillier than it had been last night, but still nothing to the icy cold of the passing Race. Her leather jacket with all its magical pockets was perfectly comfortable in this weather.

There was no sign of whoever had started all this, and she had a feeling that was what was bothering Jaxer.

But just to make sure… "You think someone really will show up tomorrow night? Or was this all some weird accident of some kind?"

"I think someone will show up tomorrow night. The Rider didn't give me much again. Still didn't know why they were racing past this crossroads. Didn't really care. I didn't push the conversation."

"I noticed. Thank you." She shifted to her other foot and the silverware around her neck clinked together, making a tinkling noise. "The Nags still aren't picking up anything either?"

They hadn't made an appearance today. They weren't the ones sending her out here, at least not directly, but she assumed that was because she was already coming out here with Jaxer, and that they were doing their part of the job, which was to research and/or work on getting premonitions that would give Cary a clue who she was supposed to be saving.

Jaxer shook his head, his gaze turned inward. "I hate dealing with European Fae," he said after a moment.

That was…interesting. "Mind if I ask why?"

He blinked and looked at her. His expression went through a series of expressions which revealed none of his thoughts and then he smiled. "They're a pain in the ass," he said. "You've met Tom the leprechaun. All of the European Fae are irritating." He kept her from asking more questions by changing the subject. "Be sure to wear your anti-Fae gear again tomorrow night. I can feel the iron from here. It'll help if no one shows up."

"None of this bothers you when it's in my house and you're in my house. Why does it bother you out here in the middle of nowhere?"

"It doesn't bother me particularly. Not like being enclosed in an elevator or car. None of it contains a high enough iron content to really get under my skin, so to speak."

She snorted.

"But when the veil between the realms thins at a crossroads like this, my tolerance for iron can…waffle a bit."

"Waffle?"

"Shimmy? Dance? Change?"

She scowled. "Ha ha. I know what waffle means as a word. What does it mean in this context?"

"That when I'm standing next to a crossroads that touches into Faery, even small amounts of iron are more…obvious to me."

"Did the Rider comment on me hiding in the car?" That would be embarrassing if it hadn't been absolutely necessary.

"No. Not everything is about you."

She stuck her tongue out at him. "Until tomorrow night, then?"

"Tomorrow night. I'll talk with Liruk and Wisat more, see if they've uncovered anything. If we come up with any answers, I'll meet you at your house first."

"Cool."

She clanked back to her car, leaving the various tools in her pockets on the drive home, but she did take the silverware necklace off. If she got pulled over for a traffic violation, she didn't want to have to answer questions about why she was wearing forks and knives and spoons strung together on a leather strap around her neck.

JAXER NEVER MADE AN APPEARANCE AT HER HOUSE THE NEXT day, so Cary had to assume he and her bosses hadn't found much to help. She spent the day playing with the dogs and pacing her house, and then finally went up into her secret attic and did some reading on the Fae, specifically the Riders, trying to find anything helpful, anything that might give her a clue what was happening.

What she might expect that night.

She had no idea if the Riders would return to their usual route—on the opposite side of the Atlantic from here—or if they would always pass that crossroads now until something else happened to change their route. She was a little worried about that happening. She couldn't be out there every night. Eventually, she'd have to go protect someone. But it would be a vulnerable spot where unsuspecting humans could get sucked into the Race. That would be bad.

Her reading didn't help a lot. A refresher course on the Riders, but she didn't learn much new, just reminded of some of the things she'd forgotten. Mostly, the emphasis on the dangers of getting pulled into the Race repeated on an endless loop.

Apparently, it was even dangerous for Fae who weren't normal participants in the Race to join. Which mean Jaxer had been in a bit of trouble that night when the Rider had invited him into the Race. Probably why she'd been able to break out of her daze, or Fae thrall or whatever.

She hated dealing with Fae thralls. Sucked you in, made you think you wanted something that would kill you, then killed you. Or kept you eternally stuck in Faery until you wasted away to nothing and then, if you were lucky, you died.

Faery had a remarkable number of ways to lure in unsuspecting beings and kill them very slowly over a remarkable number of years. And not in the usual just aging-and-everyone-dies way but in a not-eating-turning-into-a-wraith kind of way. Definitely not good.

She worked for North American Fae and her mentor in this Protector job was a High Fae, and she would never even think of going into Faery itself on purpose. The thought of getting stuck there was haunting. Almost as bad as ghosts.

Okay, nothing was as terrifying as ghosts. Ghosts were the worst. But getting stuck and wasting away in Faery ranked right up there.

When she finally came down from the attic, the dogs were patiently waiting for dinner and she was starved. She had a few more hours, but then she needed to leave. The drive wasn't a short one. And the Riders were due at midnight.

And she was no closer to any answers.

She arrived at the crossroads ten minutes before midnight. This night was chillier than the last two, even without the supernatural frost, so she'd worn a thicker shirt under her leather jacket and popped a knit beanie on her head, which flattened out her ponytail and wasn't her most flattering look but she didn't care.

Unless someone showed up for her to Protect, she'd be spending the midnight moments inside her car, surrounded by iron.

She brought the same silverware necklace as last night and filled her jacket's magic pockets with tools. She even brought her hammer. Which was heavy as hell and she never used it if she could avoid it, but her dad had insisted she needed a hammer and since he'd given her this one she wasn't inclined to get rid of it in favor of something lighter and easier to use. Besides, in this case, having a heavy steel hammer with a high iron content in the alloy meant another dual-purpose weapon against the Fae.

She really needed to get to Lucy's dojo more often, though. She had to practice self-defense for those times when she didn't have shields. She wasn't entirely sure why she kept avoiding the training. Something to do with it feeling pointless? Or she just didn't like getting tossed around the dojo by her five-foot-tall best friend who was a remarkably strict teacher.

With all the iron she could carry—and thank the universe for magical pockets because her jacket didn't feel any heavier than normal. She couldn't even feel the hammer inside her inner pocket!—she got out of the car after arriving and walked to the crossroads. She'd beat Jaxer here tonight, which was a little surprising. He was usually waiting for her whenever they met somewhere and she was forced into taking a conventional method while he got to take shortcuts he never explained to her.

She listened tensely but no sound of hooves slamming into dirt yet. A few ordinary night sounds. Some night birds squeeing, a high pierced buzzing chitter from bats swooping down to eat night bugs, a cold breeze brushing through the grass in the surrounding fields.

No scent of sulfur yet, either. Though that could be all the iron she carried keeping her safe from the thinning between Faery and her human world. She just smelled dirt and grass and not much else.

A dark, quiet, peaceful night. At a crossroads. In the middle of nowhere.

She was on her way back to her car when Jaxer appeared from…somewhere. She had no idea. One minute he wasn't there, the next he was. He might even have been there for the last few minutes. His glamour was so powerful he could make people see whatever he wanted them to, glamours so real they *felt* real. She could have walked right past him, and if he didn't want her to see him, she wouldn't have.

"You're late," she said, because his sudden appearance

had caught her out and she was embarrassed. She hated being embarrassed in front of him.

"You're still covered in iron."

"I'm a safety girl."

"That's not what Julia was talking about in that movie." He grinned, a sparkle of mischief in his gaze.

She had a soft spot for older movies, and *Pretty Woman* was a classic that she'd made Jaxer watch exactly once. He somehow still managed to catch her randomly used out-of-context references and quotes, though, which was frankly amazing.

"I'm a safety girl in that context too," she said, primly, just because she knew it would make him laugh. "But in this context, I'm not taking any chances. If no one shows up for me to protect…" She let the sentence trail off.

Jaxer didn't try to offer platitudes, which she was grateful for. "Getting back in the car?"

She had been heading that way, but the faint sound of hooves caught her attention, and under the earthy dirt and grass, the first hints of sulfur. "Think I'll hang around out here for a few more minutes." She scanned the area. "Just in case."

Something tingled along her spine, an instinct, a suspicion. Tonight, something was different. Something was going to change.

Third night. Threes.

She shouldn't have doubted.

As the sounds of racing hooves grew louder, another sound caught her attention. The slower clip-clop of a horse. Coming from a different direction.

Cary and Jaxer turned at the same time.

Along the road next to Cary's car, a single horse slowly

walked forward with a single rider on its back. The horse was an ordinary brown color, with a slightly darker mane and tail, and a black patch on its nose. Its eyes caught some of the moonlight, but were otherwise an ordinary brown. Nothing about the horse glowed in the dark.

The rider, too, seemed ordinary enough. They sat tall on the horse, which wasn't a small animal but wasn't nearly as large as the Fae's horse. In the dark, at a distance, there wasn't a lot she could pick out about this rider except they were tallish and had on a hat that was pulled down low over their face. They seemed to be wearing jeans and boots and a duster-style jacket. That and the hat reminded her of an old-school cowboy.

But she couldn't pick out any features of the newcomer until they were nearly on top of her and Jaxer. She did move a little in front of Jaxer. If the newcomer was a threat, her shield would come up and that would keep her and Jaxer safe. If the newcomer wasn't a threat and was the person she was supposed to be protecting, she'd learn that soon enough.

The tingling along her spine confirmed something was up, though, and it centered on this person.

When the horse and rider were close enough Cary could feel the horse's breath on her face, the rider tipped their head up, revealing their face from underneath the wide-brimmed hat.

It was a face that…reminded her of Jaxer. Not that the newcomer looked like him. She was darker, her skin tone a deep brown, her hair thick and black, her eyes a golden brown that looked almost purple in the moonlight. But she had that glowing, ethereal beauty, like gold dusted her skin and she radiated gorgeousness. And Cary had the same impression that she had with Jaxer, that the rider was actually tamping down her beauty. That there was some glamour at work here, disguising her true nature, because otherwise she might shine so bright, she'd blind.

So then. Definitely another faery.

She slid gracefully from the horse, dropping the reins to the ground. The horse snorted once at her, then stood where it was, watching the proceedings, not attempting to move off to eat grass or wander away. Cool trick.

The faery patted her horse's neck, then approached Cary and Jaxer.

"Why are you here?" she asked Jaxer, ignoring Cary.

Cary rolled her eyes. She was used to beautiful, preternatural people doing that to her. They always looked to the other preternatural being present and ignored the human because what harm could the human possible do. It was annoying. But she was used to it. Also, she really couldn't do much *harm* per se. She mostly just stood in the way. But for a lot of bad guys, that standing in the way part did tend to fuck up their plans so… Maybe she could do harm.

She grinned to herself, knowing the new Fae wouldn't even see it.

She wasn't disappointed. The Fae's full focus was on Jaxer and her brows were lowered over her golden eyes.

"Are you banished, too?" the Fae said. "I had not heard that. Only that you left."

Woah. There was…a lot of information in those three short sentences. Over her shoulder to Jaxer, Cary said, "You know her?"

"She was of the Irish court," Jaxer said, his voice sounding soft and thick and…emotional. That was odd. "Once upon a time."

Cary wanted to chuckle at the "once upon a time" but got the feeling there was so much more emotion going on here, her laugh would be very inappropriate and also might be taken wrong by Jaxer. So she rolled her lips into her mouth, but she watched the new Fae a little breathlessly, waiting for more information and hints. Was she finally going to learn more about her mentor? That would be a most excellent turn of events.

"I left," Jaxer said. "I wasn't banished."

His voice choked a little more and Cary just *knew* there was more to that. Like there was a dangling, unspoken "again" missing from the end of that last sentence or something.

"Banishment is…difficult," the new Fae said.

"You have been away from Danu for…a long time now," Jaxer said.

"I have not seen the face of my goddess in four hundred years. It is long enough."

"You haven't been invited back. You can't return."

"I can join the Race. I can return in this way."

Wait. What? She was here to join the Race? But she wasn't a Rider. And that was what usually got someone killed. Except that was what happened with humans and this woman wasn't a human, she was Fae, and as a Fae… Could she do that? Join the Riders and not be damaged. Her afternoon reading seemed to suggest even a Fae could be in danger joining the Race.

Jaxer answered Cary's unspoken question. "If it were that easy to get around the queen's dictate, there would be more Riders."

"Where do you think they come from?"

"No other Fae court will accept you when you've been banished."

Again, there was a rusty, deep quality to Jaxer's voice that spoke of serious emotions and Cary wanted so badly to turn and search his expression, see if she could understand what he was feeling. But she didn't. Because, for some reason, that felt like an invasion of his privacy.

"The Riders are not beholden to the usual rules," the newcomer said.

"They're too closely linked to the Tuatha to break one of Danu's dictates. You know this. You'll enter as if you're human. You'll die."

"Then perhaps that's for the best. I've been in this realm too long. It infects me." She snarled and the look of disgust was hard for Cary not to take personally. "You may delight in these humans, in rescuing them. The others…those you work with… I have never understood why they would aide humans."

"They see good in them. Things worth saving."

Another snarl. "That is their prerogative. I would prefer not to experience this realm anymore. It…burns more now."

"That means the iron in our world bothers you more than it does Jaxer, doesn't it?" Cary said. Then winced. She was supposed to be keeping her mouth shut during all this so she could learn more, not blurting things out and drawing attention to herself that might make the new Fae stop talking.

The Fae flicked a glance at her, then returned her attention to Jaxer. "I will join the Race. And if I die, then I die."

"Is your horse Fae?" Cary asked, glancing at the animal who stood passively, its head lowered slightly like it was napping.

The newcomer didn't bother to answer. "I will see Danu's face again before I die. That will be enough."

"You could just petition her for return. She would listen. It's been centuries."

"They hold grudges, the queens. You know that. She has

not summoned me. She's probably forgotten me. I will not be called home. I must make my own path there."

"The illusions you used to redirect the Riders here could have killed the humans caught in them," Jaxer said.

"They had to be triggered." She shrugged, the move lifting her duster up off the ground then dropping it back down around her booted feet. "The humans were rescued." Now the Fae's gaze flicked down to Cary. Held hers. "I chose Portland on purpose."

"Because I was here?" Jaxer said. "Because there was one of my charges here?"

Without looking away from Cary, the Fae said, "Of course. She saved them."

"I did," Cary said, annoyed at being talked over. "No thanks to you."

"I've been in this area for…a few years," the Fae said, talking to Cary now. "I knew what you were capable of. Jaxer trained you well."

"I agree. Doesn't mean it was right to endanger those people."

"And is it right that I've been denied my home for four hundred years?" she asked but without the anger or rancor Cary might have expected. Her voice was dull and almost neutral, which made it even more painful to hear.

"I have no idea," Cary said. "I don't know what you did to get banished."

The Fae didn't rise to the bait and reveal her crimes, unfortunately. But she did hold Cary's gaze for another few beats, before turning her attention back to Jaxer.

The sound of approaching hooves was louder now, Cary realized. The air had grown colder as they talked, and she had pulled her jacket closed without thinking about it. Now that she noticed the cold, she had to clench her jaw tight to keep her teeth from chattering.

The Riders were closer than she'd realized a moment ago. There wasn't much time left.

But was she supposed to stop this Fae from joining the Race, or not? It seemed like, while it wasn't a great decision since it could get her killed, this was something the Fae should be able to do or not do on her own. It was bad that she'd caught innocent humans in her spells, yet she'd set those spells, set this whole thing up in a place where she knew Cary and Jaxer would be able to release the humans. Did that make her a bad guy then or not?

Cary wasn't sure what her job was here now, what she was supposed to do. Jaxer wasn't giving her any hints. The Fae seemed determined to do this thing.

So did Cary let her, or try to stop her? And if Cary tried to stop her, would the woman just try this again?

Maybe in a place where Cary wouldn't be around to interfere. Or help.

That would be bad.

The sound of horse hooves pounding the dirt rose around them. The newcomer's horse finally raised its head and snorted, pawing the dirt road restlessly, as if it intended on jumping away soon. The fact that the only thing keeping it in place was its reins dropped to the ground was beyond impressive to Cary.

The night air frosted the horse's breath, turning it into fog. Fog that blended with the now rising fog along the ground. Growing thicker as Cary watched. They didn't have much time left until midnight, until the Riders were here.

She kept Jaxer behind her, because she still wasn't sure if this new Fae was a danger to him or not. And she desperately wanted to ask him if she was supposed to keep the banished faery from attempting to join the Race. But the question froze on her tongue.

The woman tipped her hat back farther, more of her ethereal face catching the moonlight, sparking what truly looked like gold dust across her dark brown skin. She sighed and the breath came out as a fog like her horse's.

"They approach. The third night. They won't pass this way again after tonight. This is my only chance to join the Race."

"It's not the way," Jaxer said, his voice quiet but still audible over the rising noise of the approaching horses. "Let me help you find another way. This will kill you."

"You of all people should understand. Sometimes death is the better option."

Cary had to literally bite her lip to keep from asking what that meant. Given how cold her lips were, that hurt, but the pain also kept her teeth from chattering so fair trade.

She took a step closer to the new Fae, wondering if she could say something to talk her out of this, but the Fae hissed a little and stepped backward. Cary glanced down at her necklace of silverware. Thought of all the iron alloy metals she had tucked into pockets, and held her place.

"Sorry about the iron. Don't want to get dragged into the Race myself."

"You are human," the Fae said. "It would kill you slowly and painfully. Your precautions are warranted."

"Still, I'm not trying to hurt you with all this. In fact, I'd like to help." She glanced back at Jaxer, her brows raised in question.

He gave a brief nod, though most of his attention was on the other faery.

"Right. So I think we need to come up with a way to keep

you from dying that still gets you unbanished. And we can't do that if you kill yourself by jumping into the Race."

"You think I haven't thought of all this before? For centuries? Debating my options. Hoping to be called back to court. None of it will help. This is the only way. I'll join the Race. I'll ride for eternity. At least I'll be with my own people. At least I'll be home."

"But you won't be," Jaxer said. "The Riders aren't your people."

"The Tuatha have refused me. I have nowhere else to go."

"I could… I could talk to the ones I work with. You could…be welcome there."

Jaxer sounded as uncertain about that as Cary had ever heard him. Which meant he didn't think the Nags would, necessarily, accept a banished member of the Irish court into their part of Faery. If this wasn't so tragic, Cary would be absolutely fascinated by the things she was learning.

But her heart had started to hurt for the banished faery, even if the woman didn't like humans, even if Cary didn't know why she'd been banished. Whatever the punishment had been for, seemed like it had been long enough at this stage. And given this was a Fae queen and a Fae court, the offense could have been something as mild as eating from the wrong bush to get the poor woman banished. It could also have been something as horrible as trying to overthrow Danu, so…

Impossible to judge really. But at this stage, justice had to have been served, right? Four hundred years and a faery brought to the point of willingly jumping into something that would kill her… That had to be enough punishment for most things, right?

"If I wished to petition the Fae here, I would have," the woman said. "I will do this and be done."

The scent of sulfur rose around them with the fog, and the approaching hooves sounded right on top of them. Cary risked looking behind her. The fog blotted out the fields and everything around them but the intersection of dirt roads. And through that intersection, she could just see the occasional horse leg, the whisp of a snout, the flash of a tail.

The Riders were here.

They were out of time.

CHAPTER 7

*C*ary faced the new Fae again. "What's your name?" she asked.

The faery blinked and looked at her again. Her golden eyes shining, the gold dust on her dark skin glowing even brighter now. There was a look in her expression that made Cary ache. Homesickness, resignation, longing. Hope.

Behind the Fae, her horse snorted and whinnied, its ears perked forward. It pawed the ground and shook its head restlessly, as if it was also eager to join the Race. Cary still wasn't even sure if that was an ordinary horse or a Fae horse. If it was an ordinary horse, the Race would kill it.

She really hated that idea.

"My name is Amaritha," the Fae said. "And it is time for me to go home."

"This isn't home," Jaxer said from just behind Cary.

That fact that, during this entire conversation, he'd never stepped around her left Cary wondering if he was in danger from Amaritha, from any of this. Because he was using her ability to protect him. And he might be doing that to keep her safe. But if he wasn't in danger, that ploy wouldn't work.

Her shield wouldn't come up. So what kind of danger was he in?

"This is suicide. You aren't a Rider."

"The Riders are of the High Fae. I am High Fae. I will be welcomed."

A horse's snort, from behind Cary this time, had her going very still. She carefully looked over her shoulder.

The white Rider from the previous two nights stood there atop their huge white horse with its red eyes and red nostrils, the horse breathing steam, everything about them glowing, like they were the moon reflecting sunlight that no one else could see.

Gangs all here, Cary thought, and then had to press her lips together so she wouldn't laugh out loud at her own stupid internal joke that was born out of nervousness and a low level of fear. She was pretty sure none of the Fae, not even Jaxer, would understand that laugh. And Jaxer would probably think the lure of Faery had gotten to her.

She wasn't feeling that pull like she had the first night. Wasn't feeling a need to get closer to the Rider. Didn't even see them as magnetic and attractive as she had the first night. Either her shield was up or all the iron shit she'd hung on her person was working. Whichever was helping, it was nice to know she wasn't going to launch herself into the Race.

Now they just had to keep Amaritha from doing that.

Or did they? She still wasn't really sure. Jaxer seemed to think joining the Race would kill Amaritha. Amaritha didn't seem to mind the idea of dying in the Race. Cary's instinct was to stop Amaritha killing herself. But at the same time, did Cary have the right to interfere? This was between Amaritha and Danu and was a faery thing that didn't involve any innocent victims. The innocent victims had all already been saved from the spells that had gotten the Riders here.

Now… It was like she was here to bear witness more than to stop anything. But she didn't want to bear witness to someone launching themselves into something potentially deadly.

"Amaritha," the Rider greeted. Which…frankly, surprised Cary. She wasn't sure why. "I'm surprised it has taken you this long to petition us."

"I…did not think I would be welcome. I have not been welcome anywhere else. And you are…closer to Danu."

"We are beholden to no goddess. We are our own court. We decide who is welcome. And who is not."

Amaritha lifted her chin. "You allow humans to race with you until they die. Will I be given less welcome than a human?"

The way she said human like it was a bad word made Cary roll her eyes. But no one was paying attention to her. She didn't move out from in front of Jaxer, though. And, tellingly, Jaxer still remained behind her.

"Humans are weak and can't resist our lure. It is their lot to attempt to join us and die. To fall in love where they shouldn't. You are not human. And it is not love that has brought you here."

"I cannot live among them anymore. This realm burns and stinks and I am tired."

"Stinks?" That was rich considering the pervasive scent of sulfur currently surrounding them.

Everyone ignored her outburst.

"I wish to join the Race," Amaritha said. "I will race with you forever."

"It will not get you home. We race through the realm of the Tuatha, but we are not of the People. You will not get back to the Irish court. Once you begin the Race, it is for eternity. There is no dropping out. Even to return to this human realm."

"I will be among the Fae."

"Are you prepared to do as we do?"

Amaritha paused and that had Cary's nerves tingling. She was quick to accept riding around forever, never quite getting back to her home, but she paused over doing what the Riders do? Which begged the question, what did they do that warranted that pause?

"I will," Amaritha said, her chin lifting again. But the conviction in her tone was not as strong as it had been moments ago.

"What are they talking about?" Cary whispered to Jaxer. "This last part. What's it mean?"

"Later," he murmured.

Which she understood but was still irritating. Something important was happening and she was the only one here who didn't understand.

Though, to be fair, she was often the one standing around not understanding what was happening.

"Then you may join the Race," the Rider said. They glanced at Amaritha's horse. "That is of this realm. It will not survive our travels."

Oh. Yeah, no, Cary wasn't going to let that happen. "Horse stays here, then," she said. "No killing horses. No killing animals."

The horse pawed the ground restlessly and snorted. Looking like it would happily jump into that race. But Cary wasn't going to let that happen on her watch because, while she protected everyone, she protected animals and kids first and always. No hurting animals or kids. That was her rule.

"You cannot race without a horse," the Rider said. "A Fae cannot."

That was very specific and meant humans tried to race on foot, which was something she had read about and it sounded painful and awful, but this wasn't a time to point all that out.

"I have a horse," Amaritha said, moving back toward her ordinary, non-Fae horse.

Cary automatically moved to put herself between the Fae and the horse. "Nope. This horse will die if it goes with you. You'll be without it before too long anyway. Gonna have to figure something else out."

Amaritha came up against Cary's shields, and stopped, blinking. She might not have been able to get any closer anyway because of all the iron around Cary, but Cary knew this wasn't the iron stopping her. Obviously, Amaritha hadn't counted on the fact that Cary was able to protect a horse the way she protected humans. Or that she would. The faery underestimated Cary.

"The horse is not going to help you," Cary said, trying to be kind. "You need another plan here." She watched Jaxer ease back to standing behind her, closer to the horse, but not right next to it the way Cary was. When the horse nudged Cary in the back, she took a step forward, then turned to face it, giving it a look. It whinnied and shook its head. "I know you want to run," she told it. "But you don't want to get into this race. Trust me."

She faced Amaritha again.

Amaritha didn't show any of the signs of anger Cary might have expected. She lowered her large hat on her brow and turned to face the Rider again, her long duster brushing through the fog. "I still wish to ride."

"And all that entails?" the Rider asked. Again.

"And all that entails." Amaritha stepped forward.

The Rider reached down and grabbed her by the forearm. Amaritha gripped the Rider's forearm and leapt up as the

Rider pulled. She ended up on the huge white horse behind the Rider. She was so dark against the white horse and rider, she almost looked like she sat in the shadows of their glow. Or was the shadow of the Rider.

Almost like they were two parts of a whole once Amaritha was atop the horse. Like they had always been that way and were supposed to be that way.

It was an odd sort of mirage that Cary had to blink hard to unsee. By the time she saw the two Fae as separate beings again, it was too late to stop Amaritha. Even if Cary had been able to.

"Are you sure?" Jaxer asked. "You can't take this back."

"I couldn't take back what I did that got me banished. This is better than living in the human realm any longer." She glanced at the back of the Rider's head.

The Rider was facing forward, staring down at Jaxer and Cary without any expression on their face to give a hint to what they were thinking.

Cary opened her mouth to put up one last protest, but she never got the words out. The Rider's horse reared up, pawing the air, snorting out fog from its red nostrils. The red glow in its eyes flared bright, and it whinnied loud enough the sound seemed to echo. Then with a suddenness that made Cary jump, the white horse, now with its two Riders, leapt into the stream of the almost invisible race behind it.

And they all vanished from view.

The sounds of the pounding hooves receded. The fog broke apart and sank back into the ground. The scent of sulfur faded, replaced by the crisp smells of the dirt road and the grassy fields. The stars dotting the night sky stretched out in a thick band above them. Night bugs and a few flitting bats the only remaining sound beyond the soft breathing of the horse at her back. An icy breeze brushed Cary's cheeks, but a natural coldness this time. Not the freezing air of the Riders' passing.

A few moments ticked by as the thinning between her realm and Faery thickened again.

And then it was just an ordinary night, along a set of ordinary dirt roads, in the middle of ordinary grass fields.

The Riders were gone. And with them, the once banished Amaritha.

CHAPTER 8

"Well that was all very weird," Cary said, the sound of her own voice a little startling in the otherwise quiet darkness. She turned to face Jaxer. He was staring at the spot where Amaritha and the Rider had leapt back into the Race, his expression hard to read.

"You okay?" she asked.

He nodded. Let out a long breath. Nodded again. Finally turned to look at her. "Thank you."

"For what? Saving the horse?" She gently rubbed the side of the horse's long nose when it bumped her with its head again, then moved her hand to scratch down its neck and pat its thick shoulder. The big animal shook its head, shivering its mane. And Cary realized she didn't hear any jingling with that sound, despite the bridle and empty saddle on its back.

"No iron," she said on a long sigh. Double checking, she confirmed the saddle and bridle were entirely made of leather, with probably a base of wood in the saddle, but there was no iron anywhere. No iron rivets on the saddle. No metal bit inside the horse's mouth—which she supposed made the bridle more of a halter? And the stirrups were leather, attached with more leather straps. No wonder Amaritha didn't have trouble riding. Although, Cary hadn't really thought about that in the moment. More concerned with what had been happening.

Which she still didn't understand.

"Thank you for keeping me from joining the Race," Jaxer said.

"Woah, wait." She took an involuntary step toward him. "That was really a possibility? You were in danger?" She swatted his shoulder. "You told me you were safe because all this was Fae stuff and you're Fae."

"I was safe the previous two nights," he said. "This was the third night. This was…when a Fae could join the Race."

"Which is why Amaritha didn't show up until tonight." That explained the threes. It wasn't just that Amaritha didn't want to be stopped or kicked out after two nights or whatever. She could only join on the third night.

"And why I was in danger. With another Fae joining the Race, it would have been easy for me to get caught up in it all and join, too. Thanks to you, I didn't feel the pull."

"Would they have taken you?"

He nodded.

"Then I'm glad I was here." She patted the horse's shoulder. "For both of you."

Jaxer's mouth twitched in an almost smile.

"What did she do that got her banished?"

Jaxer sighed. "She tried to raise the giants of Ireland."

"Giants?"

"The Fomorians."

"Wait, aren't they supposed to be enemies of the Tuatha de Dana?"

Her Irish mythology knowledge wasn't as thorough as it probably should have been given her mentor had a, so far undisclosed-in-detail, tie to the Irish court. But she'd read enough to know the Fomorians were supposedly the first to settle Ireland, before the Tuatha, and fought with the Tuatha when they came to Ireland. She wasn't entirely sure how all that worked into the fact that the Tuatha were actually Fae and the Fomorian were supernatural giants—she wasn't sure they were Fae—but she knew the two weren't friendly toward each other either way.

And the Tuatha had won that war. The Fomorian hadn't been seen in millennia.

"They were," Jaxer said. "Which is one of the many reasons she was banished."

"But wait… Why would she try to raise her people's enemy? What was she trying to do?"

"Save the Tuatha." Jaxer shook his head. "She thought they'd grown soft, let the humans encroach too much, let the world of iron and man—"

"Man?"

"Sorry. Human."

His quick grin, and the twinkle of amusement in his gaze, was good to see. His expression helped relaxed muscles she hadn't realized were tight with a low level of worry.

"Anyway, Amaritha thought the Tuatha had allowed themselves to fade back into Faery and give up their dominion over the human realm. She thought the humans needed to…rediscover the Fae. She thought humans should pay honor to the Fae, and specifically Danu. In a weird way, this was her way of trying to pay homage to Danu. To… reinstate her as a goddess in this realm as well as our own."

Cary did not miss him referring to Faery as his own realm, a comment that stood out because he didn't do that very often. Occasionally, she forgot Jaxer was a faery—if it weren't for the ethereal gorgeousness and the superb glamour magic. Or, more that she forgot he was *of* Faery. He didn't talk about the Irish court. He didn't talk about the English court. He didn't even talk about the North American part of Faery, though he worked with these Fae. He only ever really mentioned the realm when warning her to never ever ever go into Faery.

After the last three nights, where just a brush against Faery without her Protector shields had nearly enthralled her, she was more inclined than ever to take those warnings to heart.

"I still don't understand how raising old enemies of the Tuatha was supposed to do anything good for the Tuatha in the human realm."

"I've never heard the story from Amaritha herself," Jaxer said, "so I'm going on what I was told from both her allies and enemies. But as I understand it, she thought raising the Fomorians into the human realm would cause a crisis that the Tuatha could ride in—literally—and save the day. Beat the Fomori again, and win the worship of humans once more. One of Amaritha's allies claimed she wanted the humans ordered to put always all iron and never use the stuff again. For a High Fae, her allergy to iron is…worse than some. She really does find this realm incredibly uncomfortable to be in. That would have only gotten worse over the years."

"So…banishment here wasn't just a punishment of being forced out of Faery, it was forcing her into a realm that physically hurt her to be in?" Wow. That was a very harsh punishment.

"She tried to raise the ancient giants who've been sleeping and harmless for millennia. Danu thought the punishment fit the crime."

"Amaritha implied you'd have sympathy for her, understand why banishment was bad…?"

If she had thought for a minute Jaxer would actually rise to her baited question and give her real answers, she was sorely disappointed.

"Amaritha failed to raise the giants," he said, completely ignoring Cary's question. "She was stopped before she really got started. But the damage was done."

"She did all that because she hates humans, but…she set her illusion spells to lure the Riders here in a place she knew *I'd* be, and *you'd* be, to keep the humans who triggered the spells safe. That seems…out of character."

"She didn't hate humans as much as she hated the world they'd built. So I was told. She wanted their worship. I have to assume she thought she'd be a benevolent goddess?"

"Weird." Cary glanced at crossroads, just an ordinary crossroads now. "She'll be…? Will she die? You said this would kill her?"

"Could kill her. Might still if Danu decides to take umbrage at Amaritha finding a loophole in the banishment. But since technically the Riders are their own thing, their own court, they are allowed to grant sanctuary to a banished Fae. Technically, they didn't break rules. But it will depend on if Danu sees it that way or not."

And with a Fae queen, you just never knew how they might take a thing.

"What was all that about 'do as we do' that the Rider was talking about? What did they mean? I took that to be more than just…riding horses for eternity."

Jaxer pressed his lips together. Then said, "Part of what the Riders do is lure humans into the Race. It's their… purpose. Their…reason for the Race outside of simply racing. They steal human souls and that feeds them. Keeps them going."

"Woah! Wait, what? And we just…let that go? Let them race on to kill more humans?"

"They lure the unwary, the unwise. And…they supposedly judge the soul before allowing the human to join them."

"Judge, huh? Say whether they think someone is good or bad? And who gives them the right to do that?"

"Faery."

She snorted. "Like I trust Faery to be the judge of that kind of thing."

"Your bosses are Fae and live in Faery and make that judgement all the time, and you jump into situations because of their judgement on who's good or bad."

"First, they do what they do to *save* people, not…eat their souls. And you of all people should understand that since you've been working with them for two hundred years. Or something."

"Or something," he said with a mild smirk.

"Second, there's no real judging involved in what I do. I get between danger and someone *in* danger, and stop the someone from getting hurt. I even do that for bad guys sometimes. Which, you know, sucks."

"How can you call them bad guys if you aren't judging them?"

"Usually because they've tried to kill me," she huffed. "But the point is, even if they are bad guys, I don't steal their souls. I just…stop them getting their way. That's something else entirely."

Jaxer shrugged. Then smiled softly. "I know. Just pushing to make sure *you* knew."

She rolled her eyes. "A lesson? Right now? Really?"

"It's my job." He dropped an arm over her shoulder, then

pulled it back and glanced down at her necklace. "That weird thing proved useful."

"Did you just burn yourself on it?"

"No. But I noticed it. And it kept Amaritha at bay. I was a little afraid she'd offer you in exchange for joining the Race."

"Me?" Cary squeaked. "Why me? Because I'm human? Does that mean I have a bad soul?"

"Of course not." He actually scowled, the frown so fierce Cary snapped her mouth shut on any further outrage. "The Riders claim they only take bad souls, but the truth is, they'll take what they can get if they can get a soul these days. There aren't many crossroads where a human will wait until midnight to meet them or even accidentally encounter them anymore. Not without the human surrounded by a car. The Riders don't claim many humans these days. They're less picky because of it."

"And you might have been lured into that too? You might have gone with them if I wasn't protecting you?"

"I might have. The song is different for Fae than it is for humans, but it's still a call to the dance."

"I do not understand Faery. Or Fae. Or…any of this really."

"You don't technically have to. You just have to stand there and ensure the bad things don't happen."

He smiled softly at her and she rolled her eyes at him because there was too much sentiment creeping into the conversation and she was embarrassed for reasons she couldn't quite put her finger on.

Instead, she focused on another issue. "What do we do with the horse now?" She patted the big animal's neck, and it nudged her with its nose until she scratched around its ears, under the halter. "I don't have a convenient horse trailer, and I don't ride."

"You don't ride?"

"Nope. Love horses. From the ground. One and only time I was on a horse's back, I got tossed very decidedly into the dirt. By a horse that was supposedly very gentle. I took the hint. But I get along well with them so long as I stay on the ground." She gave the horse's ears a stronger rub and it leaned its head into her hand.

She skimmed her gaze over the empty fields and long dirt roads. "We're a long way from anywhere. It'll take hours to walk the horse to civilization. And then get back to my car." She sighed. Jaxer might be able to get around from place to place easily, but she didn't have that option. "I should have brought snacks."

Jaxer gave her shoulder a pat, but only briefly before pulling his hand away because of the silverware necklace. Or maybe it was all the tools tucked inside her pockets?

"You can head home. I'll take care of the horse."

"You ride?"

"As a matter of fact, I do," he said. "And don't look so surprised. I was born when horses were the dominant mode of transportation, remember?"

"And when, exactly, was that?"

"It's rude to ask someone's age, you know."

"Ha! Like that's what's stopping you."

"I know someone who can take the horse," he said, once again avoiding a topic he didn't want to discuss.

"Someone who?"

"People who run animal rescues. Family business. They'll be able to find a good home for the horse."

"Oh. That's great. Thanks." She spoke to the horse who was still bumping its head against her to get her to scratch it more. "That'll be good for you, won't it? Getting a nice new home without any Fae trying to race you to death. Who's a good boy? You're a good boy. Or girl. Haven't checked. Don't want to be rude."

Jaxer's turn to roll his eyes.

"How will you get in touch with these people that can help rehouse our friend here?" she asked. Jaxer didn't exactly have a cellphone he could use.

"I'll take care of it. Don't worry. And the horse will be safe. I promise."

"Wow. An actual promise?" She chuckled at his deadpan. "Thanks," she said more sincerely. "You sure you don't want me to wait with you. Until the horse rescuers show up."

"Horse rescuers? I thought that was you?"

"Ha. You know what I mean."

"You've had a busy couple of nights. Go home. Hug the dogs. You've earned a rest."

She gave him a little solute. He pressed his lips together but she new he wanted to laugh.

Then his eyes narrowed, his expression turning speculative.

"What?" she asked, instantly suspicious.

"There's something we need to talk about."

His tone was so serious, her stomach flipped. "What? What's wrong?"

A beat passed, another, then he shook his head. "Nothing. Nothing's wrong. We can discuss it later."

"Discuss what? What?"

"What you're going to dress up as for Halloween."

She snorted, and the tension that had been tightening her shoulders relaxed. "Funny. Okay, if you really are good here, I'm going home. This was more than enough Fae business for me for one night."

She waved to him from her car before turning back down the dirt road, but watched him from her rearview mirror.

While she could still see him, he didn't do anything but pat the horse and watch her drive away.

So much for getting a sneaky peek at one of his secrets—like how he intended on contacting these horse rescuers, or even seeing him ride a horse.

Her gaze skimmed over the crossroads behind him, dark but for the moonlight and the faint red glow from her taillights. As she drove over a bump in the road, the forks and spoons from her improvised necklace jingled on the passenger seat where she'd set them. Something seemed to shimmer behind Jaxer, a glimmer that reminded her of the Riders passing. She blinked and the illusion was gone.

But in her mind's eye, she could still see that ghostly fog with hints of the Riders inside it, the red glow of the white horse's eyes, the steam rolling from the horse's nose. A hint of sulfur scent seemed to whisper past her. And the faint sound of pounding horse hooves lingered in her ears.

She shivered and turned her gaze forward.

No more isolated crossroads for her.

Thank you for reading Haunts and Howls and Fairy Dales! I hope you enjoyed the collection and my take on spooky (and sometimes whimsical) fairy stories—even if they were mostly Irish. LOL. If you enjoyed this collection and are new to this series, don't miss the other Haunts and Howls collections, available in eBook and print. There's no necessary reading order as most of the stories are standalones, but there are a few series stories running through the collections, including Friday's Curious Shop, which you might want to read in order.

For those who would just like to catch up on the Friday's Curious Shop stories without going back into the other collections, you can do that too. The previous Friday's stories from the Haunts and Howls collections have been published as standalone eBooks, and are available widely. Start with *Friday's Curious Shop* to see how Riley ended up working at this…unique secondhand store.

For those new to and interested in the Cary Redmond series, there is a *lot* of reading, including short stories and novellas that go back into Cary's past, like the one in this collection, as well as the main novel series, which is up to eight books now (with more on the way). If you'd like to just launch in, I recommend starting with The Trouble with Black Cats and Demons, and go from there. Keep reading for an excerpt from the novel!

You may decide later to catch up on all those short stories and novellas that take place earlier in Cary's Protector career, some of which will be more fun after you've gotten into the main series. You can find those either individually in eBook, or most of them have made it into collections that have print editions.

There is also a Reading Order list for the series at my website and my store, which I do try to keep up to date. It lists the stories in chronological order and gives their general length, for those of you adventurous sorts who want to read in chronological order. Just be warned, I'm still writing Cary Redmond stories, and I do not write in chronological order, so more will probably get slipped into those shorts and novellas that come before the events of The Trouble with Black Cats and Demons.

If you'd like to keep up to date on any of these series, collections, or any of my fiction, you might consider joining my reader newsletter. It's primarily a monthly newsletter with occasional extras when I have a sale on or something special to announce. New subscribers will also receive two exclusive stories, one a Cary Redmond novella and one a short (and quite spicy!) story in my Tiger Shifters paranormal romance series. I also give out occasional short reads, excerpts, cover reveals, and discount codes to my store.

If you'd prefer, you can also visit my website or store for updates and new releases. You can also follow my author page at BookBub, on FaceBook, or at your favorite vendor. I do lurk on social media, mostly Instagram as I write this, so you can also find me there for a chat. And I *love* hearing from readers, so feel free to email me, too!

Thanks again for reading, Haunts and Howls and Fairy Dales!

~Kat

THE TROUBLE WITH BLACK CATS AND DEMONS

EXCERPT

CHAPTER 1

"Not again." Cary Redmond ducked as another fireball clipped over her head. "You don't think fireballs are a bit over the top," she shouted up at the ceiling then had to duck again as a dagger whispered past her ear.

Close. Her heart pounded. Way too close.

She needed to find the damned cat and get out of here. She scanned the apartment from her dubious cover behind a table piled high with unopened mail. Fireballs, daggers, gusts of preternatural wind, freezing hail, and the occasional lightning bolt dropped around her, roaring through the living room in a bright cacophony of magical mayhem.

The lightning bolts flashing in the small confines were pretty spectacular. If they hadn't been trying to fry her, she might have enjoyed the show.

"Jaxer, I'm going to kill you for this."

Normally, this kind of thing was just a part of her job. She was a Protector and literally got paid to run around keeping people safe, mostly from magical bad guys. Not that she'd asked for the job, but that was another story. It *was* her job, so she faced off against dangerous stuff because the Nags—her bosses—told her to.

Tonight, however, was not an official assignment. Tonight, she was just doing a favor for her demented faery mentor. The bastard knew exactly how to get to her. All he had to do was mention a defenseless little black kitty cat and she was done for. How could she refuse to help a kitty? People did rotten things to black cats on Halloween.

Except Jaxer had forgotten to warn her about the fireballs.

She screeched through her teeth and dove behind the couch as one of the aforementioned fireballs barreled toward her. She cursed Jaxer as she took a quick look under the couch for the cat. Where the hell was it?

She'd called out to it when she'd first entered the apartment but hadn't gotten any irate kitty responses. After her lurching hunt of the living room and kitchen, the only place left was the bedroom.

She pulled in a deep breath as she contemplated the long space of unprotected ground between her hiding spot behind the couch and the bedroom door. Once she found the cat, this would be easier. When she was actively protecting something, very little of the magical dangers could get to her, and nothing deadly would touch her. She just had to *find* the cat first. And quickly. They had to be out of this cursed apartment before midnight. Before the wizard got home and all hell broke loose.

Again.

She ducked flying objects and ran to the bedroom, squealing when a lightning bolt hit the ground right behind her. Crossing her fingers that there were no nasty spells waiting for her, she lunged through the half-open door and cringed in anticipation of magical repercussions as she fell onto a red-carpeted floor. She held perfectly still, waiting. Nothing. She let out a breath and pushed herself up onto her hands and knees, shaking her head. All this for a cat. That bastard Jaxer had a lot to answer for.

She rose to a crouch, trying to calm her racing pulse, and froze.

In front of her sat a huge bed, which she barely noticed because the naked man lying in the middle of the enormous mattress stopped her heart.

Holy shit.

He was absolutely magnificent. Tanned skin, well-defined muscles, thick, black hair hanging down over his forehead. He was lying against a giant headboard with his head hanging forward so she couldn't get a good look at his face, but his golden eyes seemed to glow up at her from under his brows. Piercing and stunning and breath-stealing.

Cary swallowed. Hard. Because even the captivating gold of his eyes wasn't enough to keep her gaze from wandering over the breadth of his naked chest, the corded muscles of his shoulders and arms, the flat expanse of his stomach. It took a great deal of will power not to follow the line of dark hair arrowing down his abdomen…lower.

The man straightened and Cary heard the clink of chains at the same time as she got a look at his neck—and the thick collar covering most of it.

What the hell had Jaxer gotten her into?

"Who're you?" she asked, breathless and embarrassed.

"Who are you?"

His voice carried a deep reverberation that made her spine tingle. Oh boy.

"I'm looking for a black cat," she said, knowing the explanation sounded inane. Jaxer had told her about Sheldon the Wizard, but this? This was something else all together. What was this guy doing here? He wasn't Sheldon, she was sure of it. But then who was he? And where was the cat?

She blinked and a black leopard lay on the bed where the man had been. She sucked in a sharp breath, blinked again. And the man was back.

"Whoa." Cary swallowed. "*You're* the black cat I came to rescue?"

Oh, she really was going to kill Jaxer now. He hadn't said anything about a fully grown man who happened to be a leopard shapeshifter. He'd made sure she thought she was after a little, harmless kitty cat, not a deadly dangerous big cat who shifted into a beautiful, naked, very large man.

The faery was dead. Not that she knew how to kill him, but that was beside the point.

"Jaxer sent you?" The man's eyes narrowed and his features took on a dangerous edge. He hissed a curse under his breath and shook his head. "Stupid."

"Hey!" She stood, the better to face his gorgeous disgust. No one should look that good while insulting you. "You could have done worse, buddy."

She took a step toward the bed, wiping damp palms on her jeans. The chains she'd heard earlier linked the collar on his neck to the headboard, which was brass and made-up of a scrawl of symbols she didn't recognize but looked like they might mean something if she stared at them long enough. He wasn't bound anywhere else that she dared peek, and the chains appeared flimsy enough. So obviously the power keeping him confined was in the collar.

"What is that?" She gestured with her head toward the thick band of metal.

"A binding ring," he said slowly, as if speaking to a child.

She frowned, both at his tone and the news. "But you just shifted."

"It's been designed to contain both my forms. Any other questions before you get me out of here?"

"Yeah, what crawled up your butt and put you in such a pissy mood?"

"Being held captive for sacrifice by a wizard and having a child sent to rescue me has dampened my day a bit," he said.

She grinned and enjoyed watching his eyes narrow suspiciously. "Child, huh? You know, at my age that's a compliment."

"How old could you be? Twenty?"

She shook her head. She'd actually turned thirty-one last April. But when she got tricked into becoming a Protector at twenty-five, she'd stopped aging at a normal rate. One of the few things about the job that didn't irritate her.

She took a quick moment to glance around the rest of the room. The red carpet wasn't the only gaudy element. Lots of black leather covered the walls and an animal skinned rug, which she was afraid to think about too closely given the captive on the overlarge bed, was tossed across the floor in front of what she thought might be a closet. A wood and metal trunk sat against one wall, red silk drapes covered the single window, and the overhead light was covered by thick, dark metal chains which gave the room strange shadows.

Fortunately, there were no nasty attack spells in here, which meant Sheldon the Wizard didn't want his captive accidentally hurt by a stray lightning bolt. That worked in her favor, giving her time to solve the binding ring problem without being pelted by hail.

Though even if there had been spells in here, now that she was officially protecting someone, she could keep them both safe.

She did wonder why Sheldon would care if his shape shifting captive got hurt before the midnight sacrifice. Obviously, he didn't want him dead. You couldn't sacrifice something that was already dead. But an additional warning spell in here probably wouldn't have killed his prisoner. Maybe. If Sheldon had enough control.

If he didn't, and was as powerful as Jaxer claimed, they really needed to get out of here. Fast.

She eased up to the bedside, still leery of traps, and leaned in close to the leopard man, trying to ignore the yummy, stomach-fluttering male scent of him as she studied the binding ring. It was a thick band of silver and copper intertwined in a complex pattern of twists and turns. Over the silver, tiny runic symbols danced and shimmered so they were nearly impossible to read.

"Oh good," she said, "a hard one."

The prisoner shivered, a low growl rising from his throat. The sound made Cary's heartbeat jump.

Speaking of hard ones.

She could feel his glare on the side of her face, but she resisted looking. She had other things to worry about at the moment.

Like how the hell she was going to get this damned magical containment brace off his neck without alerting the entire mystical neighborhood.

"You did that on purpose," the man snarled.

"Huh?" She glanced at him. "What are you talking about?"

"Don't breathe on me again," he said.

She scowled. "What am I supposed to do? Hold my breath until I get your collar off? Just relax, big guy. You'll be out of here in a minute." To herself, she mumbled, "Wouldn't have gotten this much grief from a proper black cat."

"You some kind of witch?"

"No." After a moment, she sighed and shook her head. "Well, there's no help for it. I'm gonna have to use brute force. It'll take too long to get this off subtly."

"We don't have much time. It's nearly midnight now."

"Gee, really?"

He ignored her sarcasm. "Brute force?"

"Hold onto your valuable body parts," she said and tried not to think about his exposed valuable parts. Then she wrapped her hands around the collar, easing her fingers gently under so the backs pressed against his neck. His skin was warm and another shiver danced down her spine.

"Wait."

She met his gaze.

"What the hell are you doing? If I can't break that with my bare hands, you can't—"

He stopped short when she tugged and the collar came away with a quiet click.

"I'm not without some talent," she murmured.

"Who *are* you?"

"Come on. We have to get you out of here. I just made a lot of magical noise with that little stunt."

"Hold on."

He grabbed her hand. The feel of his warm palm wrapped around her fingers sent tiny sparks of electricity dancing over her skin. He dropped his hold, but she saw his eyes widen with the same shock she felt. He inhaled deeply, and against her will, she watched the strong muscles of his chest rise and fall.

"What's your name?" he asked.

"Cary."

"Cary. I'm Deacon."

"Nice to meet you." Did that sounded as stupid to him as it did to her given the circumstances?

He smiled, a slow, deadly grin that made her pulse race. "Nice to meet you, too."

She blinked and shook her head. "Come on, Deacon. We need to move."

As he slid to the edge of the mattress, Cary turned her back to avoid embarrassing them both—despite the temptation to look over every inch of him. The sound of material moving over skin behind her didn't help curb her less polite impulses, though, so she hurried to the door to see how the lightning bolts and fireballs were doing.

SLIPPING INTO HIS JEANS, DEACON WATCHED THE WOMAN AS she peeked around the edge of the doorframe at the living room and the still popping spells Sheldon had set to keep help from reaching him.

She wasn't the rescue he'd been expecting. He'd expected the damned faery to come himself.

Jaxer had convinced him to let the wizard "capture" him, so they could find out *why* Sheldon was kidnapping shifters. They'd only found a few of Sheldon's victims—their bodies anyway. And they'd been little more than desiccated husks. The rest of the missing shifters... Even their bodies had vanished.

Wizards didn't typically go after shapeshifters for sacrifice. They were too hard to contain, and most of them didn't have the kind of magical energy an average human wizard could absorb through ceremonial magic. Shapeshifting wasn't typically magic. It was just a species trait.

Deacon knew none of the shifters killed so far had had any actual magic. He was a different case, but he was pretty sure Sheldon didn't know that. Jaxer did, which was why he'd come to Deacon in the first place, and Deacon had felt obliged to help even though none of the shifters taken had been leopards.

He suppressed an irritated growl. This was the last time he'd let the faery use him for bait. He'd been chained to that fucking bed all day with no sign of help. Then Jaxer went and made things worse by sending in this…woman to rescue him instead of coming himself. How dare he endanger someone else when this crusade against Sheldon was his own personal business? Bad enough he dragged Deacon into it.

But as Deacon watched the woman straighten away from the doorframe when a lightning bolt flashed, he realized there *was* something about her. He couldn't deny the power she must have to break through the binding ring. Yet she looked and smelled like a normal, human woman.

Her light brown hair hung in long ponytail her back over a battered brown leather jacket. She wore jeans, hiking boots, and a purple t-shirt with a glittery Happy Halloween emblazoned over a maniacally grinning jack-o-lantern. Her blue eyes had sparkled when he'd called her a child, then flashed with irritation when he'd insulted her. And for reasons he couldn't quite understand, he'd found it hard to look away from her, especially when she'd knelt next to him on the bed.

Something about her…something about her scent tugged at his instincts.

Who the hell was she? *What* was she? She had to be more than human, but none of his sense picked up anything particularly preternatural about her. So where did all that power come from?

Jaxer had some serious explaining to do.

Deacon shook off his preoccupation and walked up

behind her to stare at the living room over her head. Black scorch marks marred the hardwood floors, and a layer of frost covered one side table. The air was heavy with electricity and the smell of burning ozone.

Despite the multiple magical eruptions, the apartment was in remarkably good shape. As he watched, a dagger flew toward the bedroom, dropped harmlessly a foot from the doorway, and disappeared as if it hadn't existed.

Clever. Less clean up. And a testament to Sheldon's power.

He couldn't blame Jaxer for being worried about the little shit. But given a choice, Deacon would have taken a more… active approach to getting rid of the wizard.

Unfortunately, and he was reluctant to admit this even to himself, his approach probably would have gotten him killed. The bastard wizard was powerful. How Sheldon managed to be so powerful at his age was a mystery. But maybe that was the reason Jaxer was so obsessed with finding out the *whys* behind Sheldon's actions.

If Deacon got out of this apartment alive, he'd ask the faery. In the meantime, he and this very human woman in front of him had to navigate the bespelled living room and get away before Sheldon got back.

Deacon drew in a slow breath and was hit again by Cary's scent. Vanilla and cinnamon. And something else. Something that shot jolts of lust and need through his gut, making him lean closer to her just so he could feel the heat of her skin. He felt a possessive growl rising in his throat and swallowed it back, fisting his hands by his side to keep from reaching for her.

What the hell? He had more control that this. A lot more. He had to or people got killed. Resisting a woman, even one that smelled like heaven, had never been a problem before. With Cary, it took an effort to resist pulling her close and burying his face in her neck to soak up her essence.

If he didn't know better, he'd think she was a witch, casting a lust spell on him.

His nostrils flared. That scent of hers…

It reached down inside him, calling to a deep instinct. As he breathed her in, his leopard whispered, *Mine.*

Out in the living room, wind-lashed hail whipped toward the bedroom without actually coming through the doorway. And behind that, a lightning bolt sizzled the floor.

"Sheldon didn't make this easy," he said, quirking a brow when she jumped at the sound of his voice.

"Are you dressed?" she asked without turning around.

He couldn't help smiling at the slight panic in her voice. "Yes."

"Okay. Stick close. Stay behind me and don't try to dodge around me. Got it? That's how we'll get out of here alive."

He frowned down at the top of her head. She must have some pretty powerful shields to get through that mess. But she wasn't a witch?

He grunted a noncommittal response, and she swung around to face him. The flash of heat in her eyes made his pulse kick.

"Listen, buddy," she said, her chin tucked back as she glared at him, "if you don't let me protect you, we're both dead. Okay? Don't go trying to be a hero. Just stay close and let me do what I came here to do."

She mumbled something unflattering under her breath as she turned back to the living room, and he had to fight a completely irrational urge to kiss her.

Over the course of the long day, with no sign of help from Jaxer, he'd had to face the possibility of his own death. His reaction to Cary might be a result of that, a need to reaffirm he was alive.

But as he breathed in the heady scent of her again, he wondered…

Don't Miss
The Trouble with Black Cats and Demons
Cary Redmond, Book One

BOOKS BY KAT SIMONS

Haunts and Howls Collections

Haunts and Howls and Guardian Spells

Haunts and Howls Where Demons Dwell

Haunts and Howls and Jesters Bells

Haunts and Howls and Fairy Dales

CONTEMPORARY FANTASY

*Tombstone Wizard * The Unshattered Sword * Going Out of Business: Everything's for Sale * Anger Management * Demonic Dates * The Museum of Small Art's Everyman * Burning Inside a Stone Circle * Bored Questless * I Just Ate a Bug * Ting Ling * Sophie Saves the World (coming soon)

URBAN FANTASY

The Cary Redmond Series

Cary Redmond Short Stories and Collections

Demon Witch Series

Joan of Kerry Series

Friday's Curious Shop Series

Percy James Mysteries

Movies May Murder

Cookies Can't Crime

Diamonds Do Damage

Replicas Risk Ruin

Vacation Deadly: An Action Adventure Thriller Collection

Enjoy all of the Haunts and Howls Collections

Out Now!

ABOUT THE AUTHOR

Kat Simons earned her Ph.D. in animal behavior, working with animals as diverse as dolphins and deer. She brought her experience and knowledge of biology to her paranormal romance and urban fantasy fiction, where she delights in taking nature and turning it on its ear. She writes urban fantasy, contemporary fantasy, and paranormal romance in series which combine action adventure, the otherworldly, and a frequent dose of sexy romance.

The newest book in her bestselling romantic urban fantasy series about Protector Cary Redmond, The Trouble with Shifters and Fae Courts, sees a new direction for the intrepid Protector, her sexy leopard shifter mate, and the entire crew. Kat also launched a new novella length Paranormal Romance series that follows the adventures of a magical thief and the dragon shifter prince she just can't seem to shake—and really doesn't want to. The first six stories of the Dragon Thief series release throughout 2024, beginning in February with Dragon Thief.

For something a little different, Kat also publishes fantasy, science fiction, and the occasional hockey romance under the name Isabo Kelly (https://www.isabokelly.com).

After traveling the world, living in places like Hawaii, Germany, and Ireland, Kat now lives in New York City with her family and a library's worth of books.

For more on Kat and her future books

Website: https://www.katsimons.com/
Newsletter: https://bit.ly/KatSimonsNewsletter

KatSimonsBooks
https://www.katsimonsbooks.com

Social Media
Facebook Page: https://www.facebook.com/
KatSimonsAuthor
BookBub: https://www.bookbub.com/authors/kat-simons
Instagram: https://www.instagram.com/isabokelly/
Threads: https://www.threads.net/@isabokelly
Bluesky: https://bsky.app/profile/katsimons.bsky.social

Don't miss the latest Kat Simons
news, updates, and more!
New subscribers get two newsletter exclusive stories.

Join Now!
https://bit.ly/KatSimonsNewsletter

KATSIMONSBOOKS

For all Kat's books and book related merchandise!
Check out the store for early releases, sales, and fun!

https://katsimonsbooks.com